Morning Flower

Chasing the Prairie Fire

Book One

by
Taylor Phillips

To Melvin Billy,

This story wouldn't be here without you giving me

my Native name, Morning Flower.

Acknowledgments

I would like to say a deep-hearted thank you to the following people who helped me along this writing adventure…

My parents: for all of those emails back and forth as I was writing my books. Being my first readers and working with me on my projects. You encouraged me to continue my writing and the countless hours of allowing me to talk about my ideas.

Andrea: For being the first person outside of my family to read my book and talking me through some more proper ways to word my story.

Jenna: For working so hard on the final copy and really digging deep through all the miss printed papers. Your honest feedback was very encouraging and fruitful.

Roger: For working with me on the book cover and making my vision come to life. I couldn't be more honored to have your wonderful artwork as my cover.

Jenn: For being so excited for my books and helping me venture out for help with them.

And to my husband: For your support and being there for my crazy dream of becoming an author.

This book wouldn't be here without each one of you supporting me through it all. Thank you again.

Table of Contents

Chapter One

I have spent many generations passing on important stories among my people. There is one lesson that has become forgotten and needs to be told once again. The tale of a young warrior, wise beyond her years.

> > > > >

Alone, a crimson flower reached its full height as if trying to catch a glimpse of the breathtaking view overlooking the valley below. The blossom stood tall poking out above the short dew-covered grass. It looked as if groups of slender ruby petals grew up the stem. A gloomy mist seemed to creep along the hillside, leaving an unnerving feeling, covering everything in sight. It was still dark, and yet the peacefulness of it was eerie.

Wait, have I seen this before, Morning Flower wondered. *I think I have heard of a flower that looks like that.* The thirteen-year-old girl began to about marvel at what the mysterious blossom was called. As she tried to concentrate, she found herself beginning to wake from her slumber. *Why have I experienced the same dream the past few nights? Why only the same part of it? Have I forgotten other parts, or was that the entire dream?*

Not sure what to make of the dream just yet, Morning Flower tried to brush aside her thoughts and decided to get ready for her day. The sun hadn't risen yet, but that was her favorite time anyway. She had always enjoyed getting up a little earlier than the rest of her tribe to get an extra moment to herself as she watched the sun wake the earth and catch nature at their first waking moments. The morning chill helped during this time of the season when the valley would soon be its warmest. Since it was August, the month her people called the Berry Moon, the heat would come soon enough.

The teenager rolled out of her bison hide blanket and began to straighten the deerskin dress that she was wearing. She slipped her rough slender feet into her moccasins, wiggling her toes into the comfort of the soft leather. Today was the first time in a week that the young girl had awoken before her mother, Spring Frost, or father, Tall Oak. She quietly opened the teepee flap and peeked back just to be sure she hadn't woken them. With the deep sounds of their breathing reassuring her that they hadn't budged, she reached for her pouch and stood in the teepee opening. Satisfied that they were still sound asleep, she weaved her way through the neighboring teepees towards her affectionate horse in the nearby pasture.

Even though there was barely any light outside, she knew didn't need to see her brightly strawberry colored speckled stallion. All she needed to do was make a soft, dove like call and he would come. She cupped her hands around her mouth and cooed into the dawn darkness. Suddenly she could hear his heavy hooves tromping, rustling the tall grass as he lazily moved towards her. She gave another coo just to tease him to hurry. He came directly towards her as he lowered his head and butted her in the chest as if to say, 'Good Morning'.

She stood on the tips of her toes to kiss him on his fuzzy forehead, and then whispered in his large ears, "How is my boy doing this morning? Did you get into Grandfather's harvest last night?"

He snorted and shook his head.

She giggled and scratched him under the chin. "Would you like to come and watch the sunrise with me Red Storm?" she asked. Knowing he would follow, she began to walk towards her favorite tree.

The red roan appaloosa's head lingered near her as the two began to make their way to their morning spot. "I had the same dream again last night Red Storm," she continued to speak quietly while patting his shoulder. "Do you think it means something or that I am just losing it as Mad Loon did?"

Red Storm let out a loud nicker.

She hushed him as they snuck past a nearby teepee. She always loved that it was as if he was listening and at times seemed to respond back to her.

Once they reached their favorite ponderosa pine tree, she climbed up with ease to the perfect bare branch. She fiddled with the jigsaw-like bark as she took in her surroundings. The sweet vanilla smell of pine began to fill the air. At first, she could barely see the outline of the high Rocky Mountains that were surrounding her village in the valley. As dawn touched the mountains, she felt protected as the ridges enclosed her home and seemed to shield her from whatever laid beyond.

Looking up, she saw the bright stars rapidly vanish as the sun began to rise. It was striking to see the sun peeking over the far mountains and have it set the valley alight. The swallows had already started their dawn chatter amongst each other as the crickets began to hush. Then, dark purple began to push away the night sky and change into a bright pink like the colored stripe from a rainbow trout. The colors of the sky started to change faster than she wanted. She wished she could stay in moments like this forever. But, before she knew it, the sun was fully above the mountain range with the sky almost at its usual blue tint.

From her position, Morning Flower could see her Chippewa village being touched by daybreak and her attention drawn to the tribe, which was beginning to stir. The large herd of the tribe's horses made their way across

6

the valley floor. There were nearly sixty teepees in her village and each one's flaps began to open and close as the families inside were starting their daily routines.

Now that the sun had touched the valley floor, she realized the time had once again slipped away. Her mother and father would be up by now and her chores would need to be done. Her mother wasn't always going to be patient with her about her morning rituals if she began to slack off. She jumped from her branch, not even startling Red Storm, who was used to her bouncing off things. He raised his eyes slightly but continued to graze. Morning Flower started to leave but raced back to give him a loving pat on his side and tell him, "I will come back to check on you later. Do not get into any trouble." Ignoring her comments, he continued to munch away.

She stumbled as she snatched her waterskin from behind the family teepee and made her way to the nearby creek. As she turned, she ran right into her father. "Have you been out late again, chasing the wolves?" joked Tall Oak, whose name suited him. Her father towered over her even when not standing straight.

"No, just catching the sunrise with Red Storm," she bashfully replied with a slight smile.

"Well, you had better wash up and hurry back before your mother notices that you are late."

She quickly looked around expecting to have her mother bump into her as well. "Yes father," she replied and dashed away, leaving him behind. He chuckled as she quickly departed.

Once she made her way to the creek, she rapidly washed her sun-kissed face and tried to untangle her jet-black hair. Checking to see if any sap from the tree had gotten in her hair, she poured the refreshing water over her head. With the daybreak coolness, the water was shocking to her skin. The chilling water felt pleasant on her face as she recalled how yesterday was as hot as a roaring campfire during the sun at its peak. Although she knew that the increasing heat would not stop, she hoped that she could be in the shade during her chores today. After filling her waterskin she began to hike back to the village, slowly braiding her long hair.

Back at home, she saw her mother sitting by a campfire. Sneaking up behind her, she gave her mother a kiss on the cheek. She could see the tension in Spring Frost's shoulders ease and she let out a slight chuckle. Her mother had high cheekbones and when she smiled, which was rare, you could get a glimpse of her tranquil beauty. Though her mother was more serious than her father, he thankfully could get her to smile. Morning Flower tried to do little things to help a smile escape her mother when times seemed stressful.

With a more serious tone her mother spoke up, "Since you have been up for some time now, you can help me get breakfast ready? You can start with cleaning the fish your father caught since I already got the waterskin full for the tea."

Morning Flower looked past her mother and noticed the waterskin near the coals of the fire and winced a little. *If I get up early again tomorrow, I should put that on for her*, she thought.

She quickly cleaned the fish as she had done many times before and placing them over the fire. She rinsed her hands from her waterskin while her mother began to go down the list of things they would be working on today. With a buffalo hunt coming tomorrow they needed to make sure that Tall Oak was ready, and that Spring Frost and Morning Flower were prepared to help with anything that was brought back from the hunt. Often her tribe would hunt the nearby bison but in the winter, they would travel with the herd, following their food source closely. Since they hunted so often their tools were usually in good shape, but

10

since they were traveling away from the tribe it was better to have all their tools with them just in case.

Today her father would be helping the other men from the clan as they gathered their tools and checked over the supplies. Her father was skilled at making arrowheads and had been sculpting a lot over the past week.

After breakfast, the first thing Morning Flower was in charge of was going berry picking before the valley got too heated. It wasn't necessary for preparations of tomorrow's hunt, but it was the best time of year as the berries were perfectly ripe for harvest. Soon enough the wildlife would have picked them over, so her tribe tried to gather as many as possible before it was too late. Her mother shooed her away to hurry with her chores. She grabbed her basket and went to her best friend's, Swift Runner, teepee

As she reached Swift Runner's teepee, Morning Flower saw her friend and her mother by their fire pit. Swift Runner looked towards her as if she had been waiting for Morning Flower's arrival. "I'm off to pick berries with Morning Flower, Mother," Swift Runner shouted, leaping up and gathering her things.

Swift Runner's mother, Falling Leaf, started to object until she noticed the young girl was already there waiting silently with her basket in hand. Morning Flower gave a reserved smile and a small wave. Falling Leaf could never say no to her daughter spending time with Morning Flower. Swift Runner always teased her friend that it was because her mother hoped that her friend's quietness would one day rub off on her, but the two knew better.

The two girls headed on the trail to their usual berry picking spot. Some of the other girls from the tribe were already heading back to the village with full baskets. Since

Morning Flower got a late start this morning they wouldn't have too much time picking berries.

Swift Runner started the conversation, as usual. "I tried to talk to my mother about me going with the hunters and my brother as a lookout, but she said 'not yet' and 'it would be too soon for her to handle the stress of having the both of us going'."

"Well, it is the first summer since your father passed that she has allowed your brother to go on a hunt. It must be hard for her to take care of the two of you, plus your younger sister alone. She would have a hard time at home with your little sister while both of you were out on the plains. There would not be enough work to keep her mind busy. She probably cannot imagine losing another family member," Morning Flower replied trying to be gentle about the subject.

"But she is letting Crazy Legs go and I am wiser and faster than him. I would just be a lookout anyway," Swift Runner defended herself even though she knew she was not really faster than her older brother, at least not yet. She clearly had been frequently working on this argument to use against her mother in her head. She knew it would be difficult enough for her mother to let her brother go on this hunt, but it was a hard truth to swallow.

"Just give her some time. Maybe she will let you go to the next hunting trip if this one goes well with Crazy Legs." Morning Flower suggested.

"Maybe," was Swift Runner's response, seeming to back off the matter, hoping that it was true.

Four winters ago, about this time of year, Swift Runner's father, Burning Arrow, was in a scouting party checking to make sure that there were no enemy warriors nearby. Since there weren't enough people in the scouting party, he went by himself over one of the hills he was supposed to check. There were warriors from an opposing tribe on the other side and as they surrounded him, he was able to warn his fellow tribesmen of the danger before he was killed. Ever since then Swift Runner has run every day in hopes of becoming the tribe's lookout. In efforts to become faster, she pleads with her brother to race. Although he kindly beats her every time, she continues to try.

Trying to change the subject slightly since she could sense her friend's memories of her father's passing, Morning Flower asked, "Did you run this morning already?"

"Not yet. I wanted to run during high noon to train in the heat of the day." Swift Runner answered. "Once it starts to cool down in the later months, I will want to get ready for the winter weather."

The girls continued talking and enjoying each other's company while picking berries. They had been friends for as long as they could remember. Though Morning Flower was thirteen, which was only a year older than Swift Runner, many of the tribes' people called them twins because they were always together. Though they were close in height the girls would joke about which one was taller. Swift Runner always appreciated that Morning Flower would work alongside her and listen. While Morning Flower delighted when Swift Runner would talk for her when she didn't want to talk to people, almost always somehow knowing what to say for her.

After their berry baskets were half-filled and the heat began to be noticeable, the girls decided that they should head back before their mothers began to shout for them. The girls parted ways and went back to their families. Spring Frost was checking on her homemade bone sewing needles by the time Morning Flower returned. Her older brother Cloud Jumper, his wife Wild Dove, and their three-year-old daughter Little Duck, were also with her mother.

Cloud Jumper was several years older than Morning Flower, but he had definitely grown to be as tall as their father. They also had a sister, Dancing Star, who had married a warrior named Fighting Bull from the neighboring Cree Tribe last spring. It was custom for the husband to move in with the wife's family for the first year, but since Fighting Bull's mother was sick they decided to move to his tribe instead to help.

Putting the basket of berries next to Wild Dove, Morning Flower picked up her giggly niece and they rubbed noses. Cloud Jumper greeted his little sister by placing her in a gentle headlock, ruffling up her charcoal black hair. He would do this to tease her, knowing it would mess up the braids she had placed with care in her hair earlier that day. She tried to glare at him as he did it.

Wild Dove attempted to ease the sibling trouble that was starting by asking, "Morning Flower, could you take Little Duck for a while? She keeps getting into anything I happen to be fixing. Maybe you can see if Small Chief wants to play also? I know he is keeping his mother's hands full."

Sometimes Morning Flower would take her niece and the spirited boy Small Chief away from their mothers to give them a break. Looking towards her mother, Morning Flower asked in a whisper "Can I bring Red Storm also?"

"As long as you think you will not have your hands full enough with those two" Spring Frost replied, pointing towards the little one who was trying to hang upside down while Morning Flower tried to contain her.

Looking down at her niece, Morning Flower nodded her head and went to get Small Chief.

She bounced her happy niece on her hip as the two made their way through the village. They found the little troublemaker, as he was not hard to find. His mother was outside picking up all the paintbrushes he had scattered all over the grass. The same paintbrushes that would be needed for the bison hunters' horses. Morning Flower noticed that the boy's mother was frantically trying to pick up all the things her son had been knocking down. She was sure that it would be hard to get any work done with him around.

Morning Flower waved to Small Chief and once he caught a glimpse of her, he bolted towards his friends. The boy nearly knocked over a bowl of paint before his mother, Golden Aspen, raced to catch it.

Golden Aspen's face had an expression of 'here we go again'. She let out a big sigh which was an attempt to blow a hair strand out of her face until she realized who he was running to. "Thank the Great Spirit you came!" she exclaimed. She looked at her son and mumbled, "I love the child, but every time I turn around he has knocked over another thing. I am worried I will soon have more on my hands to fix than I have time for right now. Keep him as long as you would like," she laughed thankfully and turned immediately back to continue cleaning up.

Small Chief began to pull on Morning Flower's leg so she picked him up, carrying each child on a hip. The two children wiggled with glee knowing that they could play together with more freedom once they were away from their parents. Morning Flower tried to contain the two as they went towards where she had last seen Red Storm. The two children began to grab, poke each other, and play with Morning Flower's braids. The more they squirmed the harder it became for her to hold the already large children.

Once the three of them saw the giant red spotted stallion in the midst of a few of the other tribe's horses, the children began to wiggle trying to get down to pet them. Since Little Duck was around three and Small Chief was

20

four, Morning Flower knew it would be hard to keep them still for long.

She set them down and while crouching to their level said in a firm, low voice, "You can ride Red Storm only if you listen and are calm near him. If you are not, I will not let you ride him. Remember last time?" She was looking more at Small Chief than at Little Duck as she spoke.

The boy's face went still as he was recalling what had happened last time. The little ones both nodded their heads and began to calm down the best they could with all their bustling excitement. With a dove coo from Morning Flower, Red Storm's ears perked right up and he made his way across the field.

She put Little Duck on Red Storm's back first, followed by Small Chief, guiding his long arms around Little Duck to help them both balance. Keeping her hand on Red Storm's side, the four of them began their small trek to the outside of the village. The two children continued to giggle and when Morning Flower looked at them, Small Chief would laugh less, afraid he would be taken down from the horse. Morning Flower would give him a reassuring smile and his face would light up knowing he could continue riding.

The nearby magpies were singing their songs and the ebony, cobalt, and ivory birds flew near, as the four of them walked into a small clearing in the trees. Morning Flower let Red Storm walk around with the two children on his back for a few more minutes. Then she took them both off of the patient horse, letting him have a break.

Once they were on the ground she told them, "We are going to play hide and seek but we can not go past those bushes and you have to be able to see and hear me."

The two nodded their heads and began to tremble with eagerness. Before Morning Flower even covered her eyes, she heard the pattering of their feet scurrying to the nearest bush.

After she had waited for a few seconds she uncovered her eyes and began to search for them. Looking at the first few bushes and behind some trees, she didn't see them. They hadn't made a sound, which by now they would have. She searched some more then looked at Red Storm to see if he was giving any hints. With no signs from him, she spotted their footprints in the dirt. She followed the tracks and peered behind the tree where they led and found the pair of them holding their hands over their mouths with their eyes closed. Morning Flower jumped from behind the tree and startled them.

After a few more rounds of their game, she added a twist. "Since you were so quiet this time we are going to do something a little different. I will come looking for you but stay quiet. When I cannot find you do not come out until I give you a raven call, even if I call your name."

Small Chief's face scrunched, "Why?"

"That way if someone who is not nice is coming for you and says your name or that everything is ok, you wait until someone from the tribe calls you with the call of a raven. Just to be safe."

With a scared look, Little Duck mumbled, "Are pweple gunna get us?"

Morning Flower gave her niece a quick hug and answered, "No, but it is just something that is good to learn when growing up."

Small Chief puffed up his chest, "I am ready. Let's go Little Duck." The fearless boy grabbed her hand and her face came back to its cheerful self.

The two did just as she asked and would come rushing to her after she would make the raven call to them. The game seemed to have tired them out so Morning Flower brought the appaloosa to a soft patch of grass and had him lay down. The little ones snickered as he was still taller than them even while he was lying down. The three of them began to stroke him, trace his spots with their fingers and braid his hair. He was so happy his lips would occasionally tremble. He was loving the focused attention. The peacefulness was nice until they heard a piercing cry in the distance.

Chapter Two

Frozen in place, the four of them listened to the eerie sound. Even Red Storm was on high alert now. His ears were perked forward and he turned his head to get a better idea where it was coming from. It was a sharp pained barking. Morning Flower thought it might be a fox. Looking at the sun, she found it odd that one would be out this early in the day. Normally they came out later, closer to dusk. The noise continued before Morning Flower moved a muscle. She got up from the ground and Red Storm joined her lifting his heavy body as quietly and quickly as he could.

Small Chief jumped to his feet and stood like a brave miniature warrior while Little Duck stood behind him looking up frightened at Morning Flower. Morning Flower placed the two young ones on the nervous horse and began to walk towards the startling noise. After a few minutes making their way through a more dense part of the forest, the cry of agony was getting louder as they got closer. The four of them were all on high alert, looking in every direction. Morning Flower stopped Red Storm and peeked out from behind a tree.

Between the aspens was a fox that had to be no older than a year of age. She was wriggling on the ground, yanking and pulling. Morning Flower noticed her leg was caught in a snare. It was odd because their tribe didn't make snares like that or use them this time of year. She patted Red Storm to calm him before she began to creep up towards the fox. She knew she had to be careful with whatever she was going to do next.

The bright orange vixen noticed that she was no longer alone. She froze, began to bare her teeth, and let out a hushed warning yap. Morning Flower stopped and reached for her always handy leather pouch. She found some berries in the pouch and held them in her palm. The fox stared at Morning Flower's hand, then back to the questioning girl's face. The stress and pain in her eyes began to fade. Unable to resist the food, she stretched her neck out reaching for the huckleberries with caution while keeping her eyes focused on Morning Flower. Laying down her ears that would occasionally twitch, she flicked her tongue towards the fruit. Morning Flower placed more berries near the fox's face and waited for her to start eating again.

Hesitant, the fox began to eat while Morning Flower hummed to help soothe the animal. She glanced at the creature's body to make sure nothing sharp was around in case the fox began to get anxious again. She noticed that the rope was on the back leg. Luckily there were no deep cuts on the hind foot. The vixen continued to eat, but keep her eyes narrowed on Morning Flower. In hasty movements, Morning Flower placed one hand on the fox's back and her other hand on the rope, loosening until it was able to slip off the leg.

Little Duck let out a gasp as the young fox sprang back. The startled creature stood for a moment ready for someone to grab her, but when no one did she sat down, unsure what to do.

Morning Flower disabled the snare and placed the rope into her pouch. She was crouching, facing the fox to see if anything else was wrong. The fox stared back but made no movements. It was hard to tell if something was wrong since she was sitting. Nothing seemed to be bothering her, so Morning Flower stood and walked towards the children and the horse whose eyes were glued to the mesmerizing fox. Morning Flower turned to see that the fox hadn't left, but just stayed sitting. The older girl faced the trail and started to bring the little ones home.

As they made their way back towards the village, Morning Flower heard an odd set of light footprints behind her. Worried it was the snare maker, she spun around only to see a pair of burnt orange and black tipped fox ears peeking from behind the white aspens. Morning Flower turned back around and continued to walk forward with the horse. Trying to keep the fox in eyesight, she had her head turned slightly, only to see it bouncing behind them at a safe distance.

Beginning to enjoy their new friend Morning Flower turned and tossed a huckleberry towards the fox to see if she would catch it. At first, the curious vixen just watched the berry roll towards her and then ate it, but on the second try she attempted to catch it and by the third try she caught the berry mid-air. "I will call you Leaping Ears." Morning Flower told the fox. The fox looked up, unaware of her new name, still chomping away on the berries.

The children tried to focus on the new entertainment but their eyelids were beginning to flutter as the warm sun began to help them ease into a restful state. The fox seemed to have the most energy out of the group. She continued to follow them with vigor until they reached the village where she then stayed by the edge of the woods. She tilted her head as she watched the four leave her behind.

The two little ones looked uncomfortable, as they had fallen asleep on Red Storm by the time they made it back home. Golden Aspen kissed Morning Flower's forehead and thanked her for wearing her son out for her. She lifted her son off of the horses' back and laid him on a large pile of elk hide blankets. She was proud to tell Morning Flower that she was able to get all her work done while he was away playing and how she could play with him anytime.

Morning Flower smiled as she lifted her niece off the worn-out horse. Red Storm brushed his fuzzy lips lazily on Morning Flowers cheek before he made his way back to the pasture. Being the center of attention had taken the energy out of him.

Bringing Little Duck back to Wild Dove with her fast asleep, Wild Dove teased on how Morning Flower's name should have been Whispering Child. Morning Flower began to feel the early morning she had was setting in as well. Noticing her daughter rubbing her eyes, her mother told her, "Since you helped out so much why not take a quick nap before we work on dinner. Wild Dove can help me."

Without putting up any fight, Morning Flower went and laid down finding a patch of grass in the shade near the teepee. With the nice breeze blowing and the cool and comfortable grass beneath her, it was easy to fall asleep.

>   >   >   >   >

Immediately after her eyes closed, she began to dream of the single flower again. She still couldn't remember what it was called, but she didn't rack her brain trying to remember. She let her mind wander into the trance. Just as in her previous dreams she could notice it was on top of the mountain. The scene seemed to be the same until the mist began to clear; she noticed something different this time. The mountainside was filled with more of the same flowers along with other wildflowers covering the hill in shades of scarlet, periwinkle, and honey yellow. She noticed the sun was starting to rise. While the sun was climbing, she saw a different kind of light to the right of the mountain. Before she could figure out what the object was she was awakened by her mother.

"We should start to prepare your father's food for his trip Morning Flower," Spring Frost said as she gently shook her.

Morning Flower's eyes began to flutter open before she remembered what time of day it was. As she wiped her eyes she recalled her dream and the additional details. *The other flowers that had shown up in my latest dream, that had not happened before in the other dreams, had it? Or did I just not remember that part of the dream? And what was the other thing I began to see before mother woke me?* Before having any more time to think about it Spring Frost hurried Morning Flower along to help with the food preparation.

When the tribe began to prepare for a hunt, Spring Frost always told stories of Tall Oak's first hunt after they were married and how he nearly missed the bison while almost falling off his horse trying to impress his new bride as she watched from the hillside. Her father was not one to show off so Morning Flower always wondered why he would do so when he was younger. *Why would he act so foolish to impress Mother?* She giggled at herself ever wondering if she would understand that kind of love.

Many members of the tribe would gather during the preparation and share previous hunting stories throughout the year but the night before the hunt was always when the best tales were told. Everyone would gather around while the Elders had the first chance to tell great hunting legends and a few of the younger clan members would try to tell their own as well.

With the sun beginning to set everyone began to gather in the center of the village. There was already a low fire made in the center. Swift Runner had joined Morning Flower as both girls began to gather the food. The smell of cooked meat filled the air as they placed their dinners down and went back to their teepees to grab their blankets. Even though the weather felt like it could cook the meat without a fire in the daytime, once the sun was past the mountains a nip in the air would quickly set in.

As they began to walk back from their teepees Morning Flower noticed a shape in the distance past the outskirts of the village. She recognized the particularly large ears immediately. It was Leaping Ears. Morning Flower motioned to Swift Runner for them to sit in the back of the gathering circle. Swift Runner was about to ask why when Morning Flower pointed to the fox and whispered to her the events that had happened that afternoon.

Swift Runner laughed and said "Of course you found another furry friend. How many is that now?"

Morning Flower shrugged and smiled glancing back to see where the small fox was. Knowing there was very few tribe dogs that would be around she hoped Leaping Ears wouldn't rile them up. Swift Runner motioned for them to scoot further back as not to draw attention, knowing Morning Flower would keep most of her attention on the newcomer.

As they were adjusting, Morning Flower's grandfather was the first to sit in the middle of the circle where the storytellers would sit. Swift Runner nudged Morning Flower to get her attention and nodded towards the middle. It had been some time since her grandfather had told any stories. As everyone began to settle in and eat, her grandfather spoke in a calming clear voice.

"Many winters past, there was a great hunter in a village, but he did not hunt for only food and supplies. He hunted for sport and thought that it would bring him more honor among his people. All but a few had found him to be the mighty warrior he sought out to be. A few of his people had known that sport was the reason for his hunt and that what he did brought himself and the animals he killed no honor.

One day after the hunter brought back a large bear with the biggest claws the tribe had seen, one of the younglings could take it no more and went up to him and asked him, 'Why did you kill this bear? Our tribe already has too much food and it is beginning to spoil. What use can it be for us?'

The hunter stood with his arms crossed in front of his chest with pride. 'This bear will be a great sign to all enemies near and far saying we are able to fend for ourselves and warn those who come to fight us that we will fight back and win.' The villagers all murmured in agreement with the hunter.

'We have not had enemies for many winters and the tribes are at peace with one another. Even if a war was to break out do you really think the skin of a bear will stop them from coming?' asked the teen. Everyone looked back towards the hunter to hear his response.

'Why do you ask such foolish questions? Of course, the skin will not stop them from coming but the fear from the bearskin might.'

'Then what good does it do to kill for unwise reasons? If you killed for the skin and honor alone, are you not dishonoring the bear and the tribe, all the while making you the fool?'

'Do you really think me a fool to fend and think for the well-being of the tribe?' the hunter tried to keep his voice calm as he spoke but he was beginning to feel the anger rise in him as the youngling questioned his motives.

Knowing the hunter would be unable to resist the loss of his pride the youngling asked, 'If this is your purpose behind the hunt, why not accept my challenge for you?'

Intriguing the hunter, ' I accept the challenge. I have never lost.'

'You do not know what I will ask yet. Are you sure you wish to acce-'?

Cutting off the youngling he replied, 'Of course! What is the challenge you bring for me?'

The teen smiled, 'You are to go three days into the wilderness without hunting. All the while you are to notice the animals that surround you. On the third day, you must come back and tell us whether or not you killed the bear with honor or if you murdered it out of selfish vanity. If you are to lie or not finish the challenge the Great Spirit will show us who and what you really are.'

The tribe was all silent. Any challenge that involved the Great Spirit was one for stories, but when challenged with that great of magnitude, the tale was were more likely to end poorly.

This was the first time the hunter had hesitated before he answered. He knew deep inside the true reason for his killing of the bear. The youngling had called him out on it and in front of the whole village none the less. Then again he had already accepted the challenge. There was no way to back out of it now. 'Is there anything else?' he asked, trying to sound confident.

'No, I think the challenge will be hard enough as is. But know that the end result will be shown to us whether you return or not'.

The hunter began to grab his weapons then remembered the conditions of the challenge and tossed them to a fellow tribe member. 'I will not need these,' he said and turned to leave the village. Before leaving he turned back around with a sliver of hope he would find a loophole and asked, ' and if I do succeed what is to happen?'

'You may choose what is to become of me. You have three days to decide,' responded the youngling.

With a smirk on his face, the hunter left.

The three days began and he tried to notice the animals around him. He noticed that some of the animals had their own families while others preferred to stay alone. He noticed the hard-working nature of the beaver and the playfulness of the river otter. How the bison would stand firm against an enemy and the antelope would use their speed as an advantage and try to outrun them.

On the last day, he noticed an undersized bear cub crying as it laid on the ground. Everyone knows to be careful when you see a cub alone because a fierce mother bear is sure to be not far behind. The hunter looked around, not moving a muscle, waiting to hear any signs of the mother's whereabouts. After some time the only noise was the cubs.

He noticed that the cub was very tired, seemed to be hungry and almost sick. He looked around and found berries for the cub and placed them near the cub's face. After the cub took a few bites the hunter looked around. A second cub was not far from the first and he went to check on it, the other cub had already passed on.

Being familiar with the area, he realized he had been there before. All of a sudden in the distance he remembered it was where he had killed the enormous bear only a few days prior. Realizing he had killed the cubs' mother, he fell and burst into tears. It was his fault that one of the cubs did not make it. He knew that if the other cub were to die it would be from his own selfishness. The orphaned cub crawled closer and let out a slight roar as if to ask for more food. The hunter picked up the cub and brought it with him racing back to the village.

He found the youngling and fell to his knees with the cub in his arms pleading. 'What I did was out of pride! I now know what I have done. I have seen what I have to others. Let the Great Spirit do what must be done, but find a way to save the cub.'

The youngling saw in his eye how he felt was with a true sense of conviction. Taking a hold of his arm the teen helped him stand. 'The Great Spirit has not changed you. You must be speaking the truth. Now it is up to you to save the cub and protect it. Let the guilt hold onto you no more. You are a changed man.'

A smile was on his face as tears of joy and relief came in place of the ones of sorrow. The cub continued to cry with hunger and the hunter, who was now called The Caregiver, fed the cub more food."

By the end of the story, Morning Flower was listening so intensely she had barely noticed that Leaping Ears was right beside her nearly on her lap eating the food from her hands. She was startled when she realized what was happening. The girl handed more food and to the fox began to pet her soft auburn fur.

As the valley grew darker they made the fire large as it lit the middle of the circle. More stories were told as the night went on, but Morning Flower's favorite was her grandfather's story. She kept glancing towards him, wondering why he suddenly had shared a story. It had been so long since she had heard him share a story, but she was sure she hadn't heard the one he told tonight.

After eating, Leaping Ears stayed close to the girls and almost let Swift Runner pet her. She stayed quiet and laid behind Morning Flower keeping her eyes on the people nearby. At one point the fox sulked away as Spring Frost came by to shoo the girls to bed. Morning Flower's eyes had been getting heavy when the girls said goodnight to each other. As she laid in the comfort of her teepee, snuggled in her bison hide, she once again drifted to sleep.

> > > > >

The same dream repeated that night after seeing the mountain, flowers, and sunrise Morning Flower tried to pay close attention to the object in the distance. The flicker suddenly came into focus, as she noticed there was a fire down below the mountain. The sparks began to ignite and the flames rise. The fire spread as it would touch a single leaf and trigger an eruption of blazes carrying them to the next plant. She realized the fire was coming recklessly toward the mountain, and if not stopped it would destroy the whole forest, including the helpless flowers in its path.

Chapter Three

Morning Flower jerked awake and she was drenched in sweat. She was out of breath and her heart was pounding. *Why does this dream keep happening and why is it bothering me so much? Maybe it meant something but visions are rare for someone my age. Right?* She decided that even though there was still a few hours before the sun would rise she would see if her grandfather would be able to help. She knew her parents would need as much rest as they could for the busy days ahead and didn't want to bother them. She gathered her blanket, wrapping it around her and tiptoed out of the teepee. On the way to see her Grandfather she noticed the stillness of the village. Luckily everyone was sound asleep, slumbering away.

She patted his side of the teepee and in a hushed voice called, "Grandfather? Do you mind if I ask you a question?" There was no response. "Grandfather please, I need to ask you something."

If he didn't come soon she would return to bed, but just as she was about to leave he opened the teepee flap asking, "What is the matter Morning Flower?" He rubbed his eyes and yawned, not waiting for a response continued, "Why are you sweating when it is so frigid out? Come in, I will start a fire." Once he had made a fire and put on some tea, he asked, "What is troubling you and your sleep little one?"

Morning Flower told him of her recurring dream and made sure to include each of the details. As she finished she asked, "What does it all mean?" She stared at him as the firelight flickered across his wrinkled face and salt and pepper hair, hoping that his wisdom would be as great as his storytelling.

48

Before answering, Grandfather sat quietly pondering over all she had shared. "Maybe the Great Spirit is trying to tell you something. Many times that is how the Great Spirit will communicate with us by using dreams to forewarn us. Your grandmother had many visions."

Grandfather's face furrowed at the mention of her grandmother. Her own heart sunk a little, it was hard when anyone brought up her grandmother. He began to blankly stare into the fire and it was as if his mind had gone somewhere else. He didn't talk very often about her, but when he did talk about a memory of her he would often have a fleeting smile.

Trying to help distract her grandfather and herself, Morning Flower asked, "Do you know what kind of flower the red one was?" She drew in the bison fur lines for the petals to help show what it looked like.

Breaking away from his thoughts, he reentered the conversation. "Ah, the way you described it, that would be the Indian Paintbrush." Morning Flower remembered now of the campfire stories of the flower. Of how it had been used to paint a canvas for other stories or how it could be used for medical purposes.

He poked the coals of the fire with a stick as he spoke, "You said the Indian Paintbrushes were on top of the mountain? Maybe if you took a trek up to Eagle Mountain, where those kinds of flowers are, the Great Spirit might reveal more to you."

"You mean by myself?" she began to get nervous thinking about going on her own up the mountain.

Grandfather nodded his head.

Eagle Mountain would be a further distance than she was used to going by herself. It could be a full day trip just to go up it. She tried to persuade her grandfather for another option, "But my mother and father will not let me go. Father is leaving for a hunt around sunrise and my mother will need me more while he is gone."

He shook his head and waved his hand, "No, no, no. I will talk to them. The more often you have the dreams, the more important it must be. The nature of these kinds of things will be shown in time, but this trip could help you discover the meaning. You should pack and get your horse ready now. The sooner you leave the sooner you will know about your dream," was Grandfather's command.

Morning Flower did not move. She felt rushed and still had many questions. *I had always enjoyed long rides with Red Storm but never had taken one so long. Do I really have to go all by myself? Many people from my tribe have gone on great journeys to have the Great Spirit reveal something to them, but was that really what this was? Am I really having a vision? Even Grandfather was not sure what the dream was really about. What if it was just a regular dream? And why can Grandfather not come with me?* Her mind began to fill rapidly with more and more questions.

Grandfather noticed her hesitation, as she was talking herself out of the possibilities of the importance of her vision. He placed a gentle hand on her shoulder and reassured her, "You will be alright. You are a smart and observant girl. Just use those skills and everything will be fine. Trust your instincts. Just do not let your mind carry you away. But you should find out what the dream is about. There is a reason you keep having it. Would you rather know what it meant or keep waking up like this?" He gestured to her clammy self.

She had to admit the repeating dream was getting herself more distraught each time and it was not as enjoyable as a regular night's sleep. Plus, what if the dream continued to get worse?

"Can you come with me?" she pleaded.

"You have no time to waste and with me along I would only slow you down with this old knee of mine," he patted an old war wound that had left a scar on his knee. "The sooner you leave the sooner you will reach the top and discover what the vision means," his kind eyes seemed to ease her worries. He ushered her out of the teepee and sent her on her way. Her eyes had to adjust to the dark as she went to gather her supplies.

It all seemed so sudden. With her mind busy, she did not notice where she was going. She bumped into someone who came out from behind a teepee. She was startled because during her usual dawn ventures she had never run into any of the villagers before. She recognized the tall boy who was about a year older than herself named Wandering Bear.

"What are you doing up this early?" he asked.

She stumbled backward, tripping and falling over a nearby teepee pole. He offered her a hand, but before he could help her she sprung up to her feet wrapping her bison hide blanket around her tighter as she cautiously took another step back. Thankful the moon had passed the mountainside already, she hoped that it was either dark enough or that her hair had covered her face that he couldn't see her blush.

She was unsure of whether she should say anything but then suddenly murmured, "I am almost always up this early. What are you doing up at this time?"

The boy could sense she wasn't telling the whole truth but replied anyway, "My wolf kept scratching at the teepee so I went see what was bothering her. She has been acting strange and looking towards the trees ever since the storytelling last night."

Morning Flower remembered now that he was one of the few who had a wolf as a companion. Looking around she didn't see the wolf. "Where is it then?" she questioned him.

"She is just sitting facing the trees past the village," he pointed towards a clump of trees past them and sure enough a large wolf was crouching with eyes fixed into the dense forest.

Abruptly Morning Flower remembered that her fox friend was with her during the stories and might be the cause of the wolf's attentiveness. Hopefully, Leaping Ears had left the tree line after the fire died down. Maybe the fox would even follow her on her trip she hoped wishfully. Besides, another furry face along her journey would be added comfort. But Grandfather talked as if she needed to leave as soon as possible. She might not have time to find the fox, especially in the dark and being watched by a lingering wolf. She broke her train of thought and remembered why she was up and that she needed to hurry to get ready. Without another word, she left Wandering Bear standing by himself looking confused at what he had said causing her to rush off.

She hurried to gather her pouch, some of the food she and her mother had prepared for her father the day before, and her waterskin. She wrapped up the supplies in her blanket. Before leaving she crept into the teepee she kissed her mother and father on their foreheads. She headed out into the field and cooed for Red Storm to come. Once he came to her, she did her best to attach her blanket on his back. She began to walk him to the edge of the village closest to where she had last seen Leaping Ears. Sure enough, there was the wolf still laying there with its full attention facing on the trees with the boy she left behind sitting beside it. She tried to see if she saw any bright large ears but with the darkness still settled in it was hard to see anything past the trees.

She turned Red Storm around and hoped that Wandering Bear or his wolf hadn't seen them and wouldn't follow. As they began to head for the river she noticed someone running towards them. The stallion snorted and raised his head towards the person. She tried to calm Red Storm so they wouldn't be noticeable, but there was only one person that Morning Flower knew who would be up at this hour running. With a soft voice, she called out, "Swift Runner?" As the figure continued to run with no change, she called out once more but this time louder.

The shadowed figure noticed them and began to run towards them. Sure enough, it was her best friend. As Swift Runner came closer, the steed was unsure if he should ease his protective side just yet. He looked around, almost waiting for another two-legged person to come out of the field. Morning Flower petted him with reassurance, but he still kept a watchful eye on the horizon.

After Swift Runner caught her breath she spoke, "I thought I should get an early run in since we will be busy with the send-off for the hunt today." She looked over the horse and her friends pack, "But you look like you are going on your own expedition. Where are you going?"

Morning Flower told the short version of the events that the early morning had entailed.

"Well then, I am coming with you!" her friend exclaimed.

"But this is my journey and I need to be as quick as possible," stated Morning Flower, even though she wanted her best friend to tag along with her.

"Do you not know who you are talking to? Swwwiiffft Runner!!! My name means quick! And I thought we were friends," she teased crossing her arms.

"We are best friends but I..." she paused for a moment. Morning Flower would rather have someone else with her. So she quickly changed her mind. "What about your mother? She will already be having a hard enough time with your brother being gone for the hunt. How will she handle it when she wakes up and you are gone?"

Swift Runner explained, "I always tell you she thinks you will be a spirit guide for me. We can ask your grandfather to talk to her as well. Have him tell her what a big help I will be for you. You go talk to him while I get my own supplies and meet back here once we are ready. And do not even think about leaving without me because I will run up to the top of Eagle Mountain and figure your dream out without you!"

Morning Flower laughed and they dashed their separate ways.

Grandfather must have just fallen back asleep because once Morning Flower told him the new details about the two girls he yawned telling her to, "Get going already. I need to be well rested to remember to talk to them you know." As she turned to leave, Grandfather took hold of her once more as he gave her a hug before sending her on her way for the second time. Within minutes the girls met back where they had left Red Storm grazing. They strapped their blankets on their own backs and began their expedition riding to Eagle Mountain.

By the time they reached the creek the sun was bright and shining. The morning was peaceful as they spotted a brace of grouse scurrying through the field. They made their way across the easiest part of the stream and they made their way across the untouched valley, Morning Flower heard a familiar sharp bark. The three of them turned their heads to see a small fox leaping and bounding across the field.

Swift Runner laughed, "Do you have anyone else coming along that we should wait for?"

"Not that I know of," replied Morning Flower glancing behind their little friend, hoping no one else would join them.

Leaping Ears kept a short distance between herself and the other three as they crossed the flowing brook. The hefty horse began to become accustomed to the jumping fox, so much so that he would even watch his hooves as she came near them. Morning Flower smiled as she looked at her own small tribe making their way up to Eagle Mountain. She was glad she didn't have to travel alone.

"Do you think the fox will follow us the whole trip?" Swift Runner asked.

"I am calling her Leaping Ears and I am not sure if she will follow us the whole way, but I am enjoying her company. She has joyfulness in her steps." Morning Flower replied looking back at the fox, who was trying to play a game of tag with Red Storm. The stallion was too prideful and wouldn't play unless Morning Flower wasn't looking or encouraged him to. He held his head high and gave the fox slight glances trying to not give her too much attention.

"What if our parent's come looking for us? How would they find us? Well if we are in trouble and they can not find us I guess that would be better for us." Swift Runner began answering her own question.

With it being mid-morning the sun was starting to add heat to the waist-high golden fields. The sooner they reached the tree line before the mountainside, the cooler it would be for them and it would make the trip slightly easier. Luckily there was a slight breeze blowing into their faces at that moment. Swift Runner smiled as the wind continued to drift. She always kept her hair down because she loved having the wind in her hair as she ran.

At that moment she had walked in front of Red Storm and some of her hair had flowed right near him, tickling his nose and startling him. He began to let out a fit of sneezing and it took Morning Flower a minute to calm him.

Afterward, she noticed that there was a herd of bison in the distance. She also saw that there were a few lying down not too far from where she was. Something seemed different about how they were laying, though. Normally a herd wouldn't leave so many bison behind. She took more notice of the grass next to the sprawled out bodies, she saw that instead of the tall light grass it was a dark moist scarlet. Without knowing it, she began to walk towards them.

Swift Runner shouted, "Where are you going? The mountain is not that way."

Morning Flower didn't respond.

Swift Runner continued, "Well there is a mountain over there but I thought you said we were going to Eagle Mountain? That is Whitetail Mountain and it is farther away. Not that I am complaining or anything. I just..." Swift Runner stopped rambling as she realized what it was that Morning Flower was drawn to. They all walked with caution in case it was a trap or the animals were injured.

Five massive bison were lying in pools of their own blood. As they got closer Red Storm halted and looked around frantically with his nostrils flared. The fox scurried around the bison doing her own investigation. Morning Flower began to observe the sight. From what she could see the bison had their horns cut off. Her stomach began to sink as the stench of blood began to fill the air.

"Maybe the hunters from the tribe left early today and did not have time to bless them before they had to continue to get another one. Maybe they will come back soon." Swift Runner tried to reassure Morning Flower and herself.

It was their custom that once an animal was hunted, the hunter was to bless the animal and thank them for the supplies they would become for the village. They would then clean the animal and finish by saying a prayer to send them off to the Great Spirit clean, but these bison weren't cleaned. Their fur was matted and caked in bloody mud. She noticed their horns were cut off as well as random strips of their hides.

"No, these are not from our people Swift Runner. They would not have cut the horns and hides leaving them like this." Morning Flower started to feel her blood boil. *Why would someone do this?* She wondered. She bent down and touched a splatter of blood. "Besides, the blood is too cold for anyone from our tribe to have done this, this morning."

"I think we should leave. If it is another tribe or someone else they might come back for them." Swift Runner was looking around trying to see any signs of people nearby. Nothing unordinary seemed to be on the horizon, but one can never know in the wilderness.

While Morning Flower was searching for any signs of footprints of the cruel hunter, Leaping Ears walked behind one of the bison and yelped. Startled she ran back behind Red Storm as he perked up his ears with his lips firm. He stomped his front hoof as a warning. Morning Flower jumped up and took a wide circle around the bison to see what the young fox was afraid of.

As she passed the bison head she saw an older calf laying by what must have been the remains of his mother. He barely moved as he looked at Morning Flower. He let out a low moan and she could see the pain and loss in his eyes. The calf's face was wet almost as if he had been crying. He lay near his mother's back and began to nudge her trying to warn her that another set of two legs was near. His mother gave him no reassurance though, which upset him more. He let out a deep murmur to keep the girl at bay. Morning Flower froze in her tracks, holding her breath.

Swift Runner tilted her head to get a better view of the mysterious noise. She laughed in disbelief, "Do not even think of bringing a baby bison with us along the trip Morning Flower. I can see it in your eyes. There is no way we could bring him up the mountain!"

"What are we supposed to do, let him stay here and die? I can not do that! We have to do something," Morning Flower responded. Her heart grew heavier as she slowly stepped closer to him. His eyes widened and more sadness escaped his facial expressions. The horse snorted almost warning her to get away from the calf. "I am alright Red Storm. He is hurting." Morning Flower reassured him.

The calf began to stand, kneeling halfway on his front knees. She could see that he was covered in his mother's blood as he began to rise. She reached her hand out trying to touch the tuff of his head to comfort him. He let her draw near as if she could help ease his sorrows.

Suddenly he had a burst of fear flash in his eyes. She lowered her hand as she unexpectedly heard a howl from behind her. Not recognizing the sound caught her off guard. Morning Flower turned towards the noise and saw a large snarling wolf bounding towards Leaping Ears. The terrified fox began to jet towards Morning Flower, which startled the calf more. He gave his head a hefty swing.

One of his horns made contact with the bicep of Morning Flower's left arm. The pain surged through her arm as she clutched it, leaning towards the bison carcass.

The calf began to leap up and down as the fox and wolf got closer. The wolf began to chase the fox around the calf. With one of its bounds, the calf landed his hoof on the wolf's front paw. The wolf was howling and Morning Flower wanted to join the animal's cries as they both cringed with agony. Leaping Ears hid behind one of the other dead bison's body. At the sound of the wolf's continuous howl, the bison calf didn't stick around to mourn for his mother anymore. With his tail pointed high he ran towards the safety of the herd down the valley.

Swift Runner tried to contain Red Storm throughout this ordeal but with one of the threats gone Red Storm reared up and broke from her grasp. He stood in between the wolf and his girl as she sat on the ground writhing in pain. The wolf limped back up until it was cornered between a carcass and the raging horse. He threatened the injured animal kicking his hooves around. Chaos continued and no one knew what to do until they all heard a sharp piercing whistle. Everyone including the animals turned to

see who the peacemaker was.

Chapter Four

Morning Flower recognized the lanky boy at once, mainly because she had run into him earlier that very morning. Wandering Bear was hunched over with his hands on his knees trying to catch his breath. "Do.....not......touch .....my....... wolf!" he bellowed, as he gasped while taking deep breaths.

"We are not even near *your* wolf until it came and started this whole fight!" Swift Runner shouted in reply waving her arms to show what the hurt wolf had caused.

As the two continued quarreling back and forth about whose fault it was, Morning Flower was still crouching over in the cool pool of bison blood near the wolf. She began to scramble through her pack and grabbed a few deerskin strips. She crawled over to the wolf and began to wrap the hurt paw. The wolf ceased its cries and with its' large brown eyes watched Morning Flower as she tried to help ease some of the pain.

The girl always brought lots of bandages because she always seemed to have a need for them. She had torn pieces of her tasseled dress before during times of need. Her mother wouldn't be happy if she ripped another dress again. The wolf's eyes changed and she began to lick away the blood from Morning Flower's own wound.

Red Storm was still uneasy and lowered his head on the other side of Morning Flower, nudging her uninjured arm as if to push her away from the troublemaker. "I am ok," she whispered to him through gritted teeth. After her attempts to tie the knot on the paw, she nudged his nose back. "It is all alright." He snorted in her face with a sense of disbelief.

Wandering Bear stopped yelling at Swift Runner and looked at the event that was unfolding. "Nina has never let anyone else pet her," he stated in awe.

"Are you talking about the wolf? Well, Morning Flower has every animal falling over her before too long. So you better keep a close eye on your wolf friend," snapped Swift Runner not giving up on the fight.

The wolf, Nina, didn't let out a whimper while Morning Flower bandaged her paw. After it was wrapped Nina rested her head on Morning Flower's lap. Leaping Ears must have felt left out; she sulked as she came out from behind the bison, and maneuvered herself under Red Storm's legs. She hid her face from the intruders by sitting behind Morning Flower, pouting. This time the wolf left the fox alone.

"This is the craziest thing I have ever seen." Wandering Bear said in shock.

"This happens all the time, so either get your wolf and leave or get used to it. Either way, we have a quest, so no more holding us up," fired off Swift Runner. When the boy didn't move from his spot, Swift Runner told him, "You can go now!"

Wandering Bear was getting the sense that he should tread lightly. He tried to explain, "I did not mean it in a bad way but look at them! There was a calf just here and it looks like a girl, a wolf, a fox, and a horse are sitting, covered in blood and surrounded by dead bison. You have to admit it is a little odd."

Swift Runner looked at them and she gave a quiet giggle as she saw them all through his eyes, but she refused to agree with him just yet. "What are you doing here? Are you following us?" She got riled up all over again.

Morning Flower became more aware of what was going on and stopped petting the three animals near her.

She began to listen to the conversation, or the argument, that was going on.

"Nina, my wolf, ran away after I talked to you earlier and I had to go after her," he motioned to Morning Flower. "Funny things have been happening outside of the village and I could not risk anything happening to her. I followed her trail and it led me here. I do not know what it was she was after. You are bleeding, a lot. Are you alright?" Wandering Bear stepped towards Morning Flower. He seemed concerned but Swift Runner kept her guard up and stepped between him and her friend.

By the time she started cleaning her own wound, the blood had dripped down towards her wrist. Morning Flower tried ripping some of the thick deerskin tassels from her pack for herself, as she did so she noticed something next to her leg. It was oddly perfectly round. What she thought was a rock didn't feel the same as one. When she picked it up it didn't have the same texture or look the same as any pebble she had seen before.

Swift Runner rushed to her friend's side and used her waterskin to clean the wound and then wrap it in the dressing. Slightly distracted by the yanking of her arm, Morning Flower pushed away her thoughts on the object for now. She reassured her friend, "I'm fine, thank you. I think I know why Nina followed us."

As Morning Flower began to explain, Swift Runner stopped wrapping her arm and was in shock that Morning Flower was speaking to the boy. She had rarely seen her best friend talk to anyone besides those in her family or the small children she watched.

"Last night during the stories, Leaping Ears, the fox, was sitting next to us. Today we left on our trek, Leaping Ears followed and I guess so did Nina." The fox nuzzled

Morning Flower as if to taunt Nina that she couldn't get to her.

"How come the fox is so fond of you? She cannot be your Spirit Guide because you are supposed to go on those quests alone," Wandering Bear asked as he looked at the group. "So what did you do? Raise her so she thinks you are her mother or something? And why are you all out here when the hunt send-off was today. Did you not have to send away your brothers or fathers?" Wandering Bear inquired.

Swift Runner was about to start yelling at him again when Morning Flower gave a nudge to calm her down. "You ask many questions. Why does it matter to you? Oww!" Morning Flower winced as her best friend tightened her bandages a little tighter than necessary.

"Stop talking, we need to get rid of him," Swift Runner tried to speak for only the two girls to hear while not moving her lips.

The boy was unsure of what the girl had mumbled but answered the injured girl's question, "Because you are sitting in a puddle of bison blood, not seeming to mind it and those bison were not killed by our hunters."

Morning Flower clutched the weighted object she had found in her hand. She was curious, "How do you know that?" Wandering Bear pointed back towards home and said, "They had not left yet by the time I did. So they could not have killed any yet or left them behind like that. You do not seem likely to have killed them; which means someone we do not know did, but you look like you already thought of that. So that still leaves the question as to what you are doing? Besides, I told you why I am out here. What harm is it for you to tell me?"

The girls looked at each other and this time Morning Flower let Swift Runner talk. "We have our own reasons but since you did tell us why you are here I guess it is fair to tell you what we are doing. Morning Flower has questions for the Great Spirit and her grandfather told us to start where the Indian Paintbrush flowers grow. Her reasons are up for her to share." Swift Runner tried to be vague while glaring at Morning Flower, "which she *does not* have to tell you." Giving a slight hiss in her words.

Wandering Bear was confused with all that he had stumbled into. He had just come to find Nina but now he knew he had to help the girls on their journey. While the two girls seemed to be having an unspoken conversation he interrupted it, "I think I should go with you. After seeing these bison it might be safer having another set of eyes around. Plus I do not know if I could pull Nina away from you right now," nodding his head towards the wounded wolf.

Morning Flower smiled as she petted her newest furry friend.

"We will be able to handle ourselves just fine. You do not have to prove you are a brave warrior for your honor," Swift Runner snipped; she wasn't going to have him join them. It had been too odd enough that he had followed them so soon after they left.

Morning Flower flicked her friend's arm and mouthed, "Stop it. Be nice."

He stood a little straighter as he spoke, "I trust you can take care of yourselves whether it is running or making the animals 'dote' over you. You will be safe on your own. I just cannot let you go by yourself after seeing all of this." He pointed at the stained ground while he spoke and continued pointing to each of the lost bison. "Besides I will just follow Nina and it does not look like she is willing to leave. So either let me come with you or have me following behind you. It would be shameful to leave you behind if you needed my help."

The girls each thought about it for a brief second before answering. Swift Runner remembered she had done the same thing earlier when she saw her friend all packed and ready to go. She didn't let her friend go on by herself. Even though she wasn't sure of how he would help, she sighed. This would be one of the rare times when Swift Runner would step back to let Morning Flower make her own choice for them. "This is your trek. It should be up to you." Swift Runner whispered Morning Flower with a hint of guilt for taking charge.

Morning Flower took some time thinking about it while looking around at everyone's faces. As she looked at Nina's face she knew that an incident like that wouldn't happen again and she was sure she could get Nina and Leaping Ears to be at peace with each other soon enough. The lively fox was itching to come along for the journey and she could tell Red Storm was still a little anxious about all the events.

As she looked at Swift Runner she could see a hint of blame as if she felt sorry for trying to take over her quest. Morning Flower knew the decision was hers and hers alone to make.

She looked at Wandering Bear trying to see what she could read from his eyes. She saw sincere concern from him, but before she looked too long in his eyes, she looked away. She had to admit even though it was odd company she could use all the help she could get figuring out these dreams.

Lastly as she, glanced at the field, seeing all the pain that had happened at this spot, she wondered if it was the only hurt or first of many they would find along the journey. She thought back to all the unusual things that had been happening lately; the snare on Leaping Ears, the dead bison, her dreams, and the fact that Nina had led Wandering Bear there after seeing him at dawn was a bit unusual as well. She focused her attention back to the older boy, "You can join us."

"Great! I will be able to find my own food and take care of Nina if she will let me. Should we start now?" he asked. Wandering Bear reached out his hands to help the girls up but Swift Runner ignored him and stood by herself, then helped Morning Flower stand as well.

Trying not to stand too quickly Morning Flower placed her hand on the corpse. "But before we move on, do either of you know what this is?" She opened her palm and the perfect sphere rolled in the dirt of her hand. The other two stared blankly at the strange object.

"Not a clue," baffled Swift Runner.

"Where did you find it?" Wandering Bear asked.

Morning Flower pointed near the unfortunate bison's head where she was just sitting. She gazed into the glazed over eyes of the dismembered body and decided she had had enough of being in this morbid field. "Never mind, let's start moving," she muttered trying to start leading the newly formed group. She placed the object into her pouch to look at later.

"Your mom is not going to be happy about your dress," Swift Runner said as she looked at her friend's bloodstained body.

The group of six began their trip across the valley. The incident had taken away more time than Morning Flower had thought the original bison inquiry would take. The sun was higher than she had hoped. Nervously she tried to put on a brave face as if she knew what she was doing. Whenever Swift Runner had led the two girls on a trip, she seemed to at least look like she was prepared for anything.

After her new injury Morning Flower decided to rest and ride Red Storm, mainly because he kept nudging her shoulder like he does when he wants to go for a ride. After some help from Swift Runner, she clumsily straddled the horse. Once she was on him and playing with his mane he started to calm down. Although he kept an extra cautious eye on Wandering Bear and Nina, so did Swift Runner.

When Morning Flower began to ride her defensive steed she offered for Swift Runner to ride as well, but she refused. She was used to being the youngest in a group and often tried to show she was worth keeping around. This time she was trying to show Wandering Bear she was capable of taking care of the group. Not that the boy needed it.

When Nina first stood up she tried to follow the newly formed clan. Her paw was still sore from having a few hundred pound calf step on her just a few minutes prior. Wandering Bear lifted Nina over his shoulders so she would be able to make the journey without having to limp. She would have walked up the mountain the whole way if Wandering Bear didn't pick her up. She surrendered once he placed her on his shoulders and thankfully licked his ear before she pouted a little over her situation.

Leaping Ears was as cheerful as ever again, almost as if nothing had happened. She began to skip ahead of them, bouncing amongst the tall waving grass.

Once everyone was ready Morning Flower nudged Red Storm to lead the way.

The boy looked towards the direction they were facing and asked, "So where are we heading?"

Swift Runner refused to answer any of his questions, still unhappy about his presence.

Morning Flower spoke up, "We are heading to Eagle Mountain."

Wandering Bear looked towards the mountain that was not far ahead of them and seemed to accept the challenge without a grumble.

For a while, the silence seemed to make everything a bit edgy. It was made clear when they had met in the valley that Swift Runner didn't want Wandering Bear to join them. Now that he was with them she tried to respect what Morning Flower decided, and for one of the few times in Swift Runner's life, she became the quiet one.

By the time the sun was in the middle of the sky, they had already started up the mountain trail. Few people made it up this mountain often, but many animals would travel from the safety of the trees down to forage food in the valley daily. The terrain they were on was not too steep and was easy enough to maneuver, whereas across the ridge they spotted a herd of Bighorn sheep on much more rocky and challenging landscape. A few rams were butting heads as many of the ewes ignored them, continuing to graze on any vegetation in the soothing shade of the ridges.

Wandering Bear was the one who broke the silence again, "So, you said your grandfather told you to go to the top of Eagle Mountain for the Great Spirit to reveal something to you. What are you searching for?"

"You should start with an easier question?" Morning Flower joked.

"Oh ok. Is Leaping Fox your Spirit Guide?" he asked.

"It is Leaping Ears and no I do not think so. We only met yesterday."

Wandering Bear in wonder replied, "Really? I have never seen a fox act like that around people." At that moment Leaping Ears sprinted ahead of them, turned and sat waiting for the rest of them to catch up.

"My niece, her friend and I found her in the woods yesterday caught in a snare. She has been following me ever since I freed her." Morning Flower smiled at Leaping Ears. The fox did look much happier today than when they had first met.

"Did you save your horse from a snare too? He is quite protective of you," Wandering Bear asked with a sheepish grin. Red Storm snorted at the boy whenever he looked back. Nina bared her teeth in response but the boy patted the wolf's nose to calm her down.

She stroked her horse's neck, "No. He is the foal of my father's horse. We named him Red Storm because when he was a colt, my brother and father would fight practice battles with me and one time I had tripped. He rushed over like he did today and began to rear up, telling my brother and father off. Though he is gentle with me, whenever something happens to me he is the first one to respond like a raging furry red storm. He and Swift Runner, I should say. She is always there for me too".

Swift Runner had been walking ahead and overheard Morning Flower say this about her. She turned to see her friend's face and blushed that Morning Flower would say such a nice thing about her to a stranger.

Morning Flower began to speak with ease, "One time a few winters ago one of the boys from the tribe pushed me down and began to call me Mouse. He told me to talk, he pushed and tripped me. Before my older brother could hit the boy, Swift Runner punched him in the cheek. He never called me that again." The three of them laughed thinking about the story.

"I will remember not to call you that," Wandering Bear stated.

They came to a bend in the trail and heard a creek nearby. They agreed to stop for a break. Even though Swift Runner tried not to act tired and said that she could continue walking for hours, she was relieved when they stopped to rest.

Morning Flower fumbled as she slid off of the horse's back with her one good arm trying to do so by herself. She led him to the babbling creek where Morning Flower and Swift Runner refilled their waterskins.

All of them took their time lapping up the freshwater. Even with the shade of the trees, it was most likely cooler than the valley but the heat mixed with the hike seemed to add to the temperature.

Wandering Bear had taken Nina off from his shoulders and laid her near the stream. Even though the wolf was nearly the size of the boy, he didn't complain once during the trip. She dipped her head into the water to cool herself down. With all the additional fur Red Storm, Leaping Ears and Nina had, they were starting to enjoy the stream more and more. Leaping Ears was trying to catch a frog that kept hopping out of her reach. Red Storm didn't mind her splashing the water all around him. He stood with his hooves completely immersed in the water and drank away.

"I have been told of a clear lake near the top of the mountain. That will be nice once we arrive," said Wandering Bear.

Morning Flower began to wonder what they were to do once they reached to top as she dipped her head into the river to wet her hair and braided it. A trickle of the cool water fell down her neck and gave her chills and let her forget about the top of the mountain for a moment. She began to wash her face and arms trying to continue cooling off. The refreshing water began to bring some extra energy to everyone.

Then Red Storm threw his vanity away and plopped down into the creek and began to roll in the water. After his cool down, he got back up, flipping his long mane and stood with his usual prideful self acting as if nothing had happened.

Once some more time had slowly passed at the creek, Morning Flower grabbed some of the food in their pouches. Both girls offered some to Wandering Bear but he refused. He got up and went to a berry bush a little ways off the trail. As the three ate, Red Storm began to graze on the grass surrounding them. Leaping Ears recognized the pouches and skipped towards Morning Flower begging for some. On her way, Wandering Bear tossed a berry, from the bush he was at, towards her. Her eyes lit up as she saw the full bush and sped over to join him. As she got closer she began to be wary of him and trotted to the far side of the bush, just in case he thought of stealing her berries.

Morning Flower checked her bandages as she was sitting. As she peeled off the leather strips she saw that the gash was mostly dried up. She cleaned the wound and the bandage in the creek. Setting the bandage on a heated rock to dry off she began to look for some nearby herbs that would help the slash heal quicker. Now that the bleeding had stopped and been cleaned, it was easier to see what the grieving calf had done.

The cut took up a majority of her upper arm. Luckily it was wider than it was deep, but it was still a major wound. She would make some Wakinakim poultice once they reached the top of the mountain to help with the swelling and pain. Hopefully, the bushes she would need would be near the top.

Taking notice of the injury Wandering Bear spoke, "You should call the bison calf Thundering Hooves for when you have to tell of the reason you have a scar on your arm," said Wandering Bear.

"Or Raging Horns," Swift Runner replied.

For now, Morning Flower tried not to think about the heartbroken calf. She continued to clean herself and once the bandage had dried, she re-wrapped her arm trying not to bring attention to herself.

Though this was the time of day that Morning Flower would usually try to sneak a nap she knew they needed to continue on. She tried to look out past the trees. She could barely see the village from that distance but she guessed they had to be close to halfway up the mountain. Wandering Bear and Swift Runner noticed Morning Flower getting ready and they began to prepare themselves as well.

Morning Flower asked, "Swift Runner did you want to ride Red Storm for awhile? I need to stretch my legs." She also needed to get her mind off the aches of her arm.

This time, knowing they still had a ways to go, Swift Runner said, "Only for a little bit." And with that, she hopped onto the horse.

"Come on Leaping Ears," called Morning Flower. The fox turned with her face full of berries and the fur around her mouth purplish blue. She trotted to the creek and took another drink then began to follow the herd.

It didn't take long for everyone to dry up from their rest. On top of the horse, Swift Runner got a better look at her best friend's dress that was bloodstained. Realizing that they still had left a few questions unanswered she asked, "You said that our tribe had not left yet. So do you have any clues to who could have done that to the bison down in the valley?"

Wandering Bear readjusted the wolf on his shoulders before answering, "No. I do not think anyone from any tribe would have done that but it was not another animal either because the horns were cut."

"Do you think they were sick and died? Then maybe someone tried to use pieces of them as resources?" Swift Runner was trying to create more positive thoughts than thinking someone was killing them that way on purpose.

Morning Flower started to feel sick at the thought of the earlier events. She was usually the more encouraging between the two girls but this was one of the more difficult things she had seen. Sadly she replied, "I don't think that's what happened." The group went back to its noiseless state.

After some time being back on the trail Red Storm, Leaping Ears, and Nina began to get anxious. Their ears were constantly focused. Twitching at every sound and their heads would whip into the direction anytime they heard a branch break or a bush rustled. Noticing the animals' unusual jumpiness Morning Flower began looking for any signs of their uneasy behavior. Nothing seemed to stand out until she almost stepped on a perfect animal paw print. She stopped walking and looked down. It was a mountain lion's paw print.

She immediately looked up into the nearest Ponderosa Pine trees. With these high branches, they would be easy for the lion to climb and wait for prey to walk past along the trail. As her eyes scoured the trees for any more signs Red Storm stopped walking not wanting to leave his girl behind. Leaping Ears, who was further ahead, spun around and raced to the protection of the pack. Even though Nina was still on Wandering Bear's shoulders, she held her head up high and began to sniff the air. The wind was blowing towards them so if the mountain lion was ahead of them it would have no notice of their scent.

"What is it?" asked Swift Runner.

Morning Flower pointed to the paw print. Not noticing any signs of the unseen animal that made it, they all quickened their pace with an unspoken agreement.

Chapter Five

Noticing a small herd of mule deer up ahead everyone began to relax. If the undisturbed deer were only bothered by them trespassing, then the mountain lion must have been further away than they had originally thought. They began to go back to their original pace and walked with ease.

"So how did you get Nina?" Swift Runner asked.

"A few winters ago I found her lying half dead in a snowbank. She must have been in a fight with another animal. I thought she was already gone and went to bless her when she tried to lick my hand. I had to help her so I dragged her and snuck her into the village. My mother healed her and taught me how to care for her wounds. Once her health improved my mother told me it was time to let her go back with her own pack. But when I brought her outside the village to release her, she sat there and looked at me with confusion. I turned to leave her there and she rushed up to me and gently bit on my sleeve. It was as if she did not want to go back anymore. I never tied her up in case she wanted to leave but she always stayed nearby." Wandering Bear replied while scratching under her chin.

Swift Runner's suspicious questions began to flow, "If you were going to let her go, why did you not let her go by herself this morning?"

Wandering Bear thought about it for a moment before responding, "I guess I knew something was off. So I wanted to check on her. I thought even if she left, I wanted to make sure she ended up in good care."

Morning Flower looked at Leaping Ears. She understood what he had meant. She had tried to do the same for each creature she crossed paths with. She began to wonder if there would come a day when the fox would just disappear.

"Wait you said that she had never let anyone pet her before. Does she let your family pet her?" Swift Runner asked.

"No. She tolerates them and they respect her but she had only let me pet her head. She even rarely lays her head on me."

Swift Runner cautiously looked at the wolf's jaws as Nina was panting and asked, "Has she ever, you know... bit anyone?"

Wandering Bear continued walking with pride as he spoke with confidence, "Never! Not even when people have threatened her. She just stands her ground but will not move. That is why I was worried about her leaving."

"Have you seen her get hurt by people before?" Swift Runner asked.

The boy looked with a wounded expression up at the wolf on his shoulders. His tone changed as he replied, "Yes." He ruffled the fur near Nina's cheek and she let out a toothy smile.

Swift Runner looked over at Morning Flower with her eyebrows raised. She was about to ask if he had hurt her but then felt ashamed at the face of disappointment that Morning Flower returned to her.

They were about to reach the top of the mountain where the lake was when they heard an alarm of hollow toots. The group halted in their tracks and began to inquisitively look around. The curious fox began to walk in a direction that took her off of the trail and stopped behind a tree. Morning Flower walked around with caution only to discover a small screech owl with large eyes, who had her wing caught in a branch. The gray owl, with black speckles, began to call out a louder alarm seeing that she was being surrounded.

Morning Flower bent down and tried to soothe the owl, but she heard a startling warning call from behind her. The little owl's partner came promptly swooping in. After he landed, he stood between Morning Flower and his injured love. Even though he barely stood a foot off the ground, he fought with vigor. With his wings spread wide, he tried to peck any time Morning Flower moved her hands towards the two. Feeling that he had protected his sweetheart well so far against such a dangerous looking clan, he puffed up his chest more and began to flap his wings.

There was a moment while he was hopping onto a nearby small rock and as he used his wings to balance and

Morning Flower gently grabbed him. She was struggling to contain him as her arms' pain began to act up again. In her hands, he began to peck and bite trying to free himself. Morning Flower exclaimed to him, "Just one moment!"

Swift Runner was down from Red Storm by now and came to hold the feisty owl for her best friend. Once they made the pass of the captured owl, for a brief moment he stopped his fight to see if Morning Flower was going after his sweet. He began to struggle even more the closer she got.

Morning Flower untangled the poor little owl's wing from the bramble and held her softly. The little female owl hummed to ease the stress her mate was feeling. He slowly began to bite less but gave Swift Runner the evil eye. She placed him on the ground while Morning Flower examined his mate's wing. Placing the injured tiny owl next to the other, she nuzzled her beak under his chin. He looked almost torn that he wasn't able to stop the two legs but was also glad they were helping her.

They doted upon each other for a moment until he inspected the wing himself. He nudged her wing with his beak. Then stepping back he began to flap his wings and she mirrored him. When she was unable to lift off, she stopped and returned to snuggling him. Morning Flower picked the two screech owls up and began to make her way to the trail.

"Wait? What are you doing?" asked Wandering Bear as she continued to walk further.

"It will be getting dark soon. We will set up camp at the lake and they will rest with us. It is not safe to leave them alone on the forest floor especially at night," Morning Flower responded.

He started, "But…"

Morning Flower interrupted him, "Do not worry. It is just for the night. She just needs to rest her wing just like Nina needed to rest her paw today. Once the soreness is gone it will be easier for her."

Swift Runner told him, "There is no use arguing with her when it comes to animals. Her mind is set, we should just keep walking."

The eight of them began to make their way to the lake: three traveling teenagers, a protective horse, a playful fox, a strong wolf, and two lovestruck owls.

Within the hour they all arrived at the sparkling lake safe and sound, though almost half of them were injured. The clearing seemed like a safe haven, peaceful and still. There was a calming meadow before reaching the lake where the knee-high grass swayed gently in the breeze.

With the green pasture and water surrounding them, the air had a less dusty taste on their tongues.

Wandering Bear laid Nina down near the lake and she began to lap up the water. After her refreshing drink, she braced herself as she put weight on her front paw. She stood for the first time since the incident that had happened earlier that day. She stretched and tried walking around a little until she found a soft patch of grass to lay back down in.

Red Storm immediately began to graze as soon as he saw the luscious meadow. For the first time, the energy-filled Leaping Ears laid down to rest. She curled up near Nina and was quickly taking a nap. Morning Flower placed the two owls in the grass not too far from the inactive fox and the wolf. Neither of which bothered the owls, being too tired from their all day trip. The larger owl kept his eyes carefully watching the group during their activities. The little owl began to clean the larger owl's feathers, looking as if she was giving him small kisses.

With all of the animals settling in so easily, Morning Flower filled her waterskin and began to look around the area. She looked past the tranquil lake, it looked similar to the side they were on, a clearing before the forest began. To her left, she saw the ground increase its height to a more rigid state. She thought it would be a good time to explore the area by herself and fumbled, "I'm going up on that ridge for a little bit to um....figure things out."

Before Wandering Bear could offer assistance to her idea, Swift Runner replied, "That is ok. We will set up a camp for the night while you are... up there." Swift Runner knew Morning Flower would need to be by herself if the Great Spirit was going to reveal anything to her. So she decided she would give Wandering Bear chores to keep him busy.

"But I…" Wandering Bear started but Swift Runner interrupted.

"I need your help setting up camp." She raised her eyebrows trying to have him ease off the subject.

The boy still wasn't sure what all was going on with the girls even after spending the whole day with them, but he let it go.

Red Storm raised his head as Morning Flower began to leave. She patted his head as to assure him she would be safe if he rested while she was gone.

Morning Flower made her way to the top of the ridge. She realized this was the first time she had been alone since dawn. Her mind began to mosey over the day's events and she wondered if a revelation would happen once she reached a certain spot. *Will I just know or will I have another vision?* She wished she had been able to ask

Grandfather more questions about how the Great Spirit reveals what the dream means.

She was close to exhaustion when she finally made it to the top. From where she stood she could see her own and the neighboring Cree village each on the opposite sides of Eagle Mountain. The view was breathtaking. As she sat down she realized she was sitting in a pasture covered in wildflowers and Indian Paintbrushes. She brushed her fingers on one of the ruby colored flowers she had seen from her dream. *The Great Spirit must have something to show me,* she thought to herself.

She had a mixture of excitement and nervousness begin to flutter in her stomach as she closed her eyes, beginning to wait, after about a half an hour nothing happened. She opened her eyes as she looked around trying to notice any small detail to give her a hint. The sun would be setting shortly and she felt she had to get her answers soon. She forced her eyes shut and prayed silently. *Please*

Great Spirit! What is it that you want me to know? What am I missing? I came to the mountain with the paintbrushes, why are you not telling me? She took a deep breath. Peeking with one eye open she tried to see if anything new was to be discovered. *Anytime now.*

There was no change, only the display of colors in the sky beginning to make its nightly ritual of good nights. The flowers surrounding her began to tuck in their petals waiting for the sun's return in the morning.

Feeling pressed for time she prayed faster now but this time out loud, "Please!! Show me something! This is where you wanted me to be right? Why would you keep sending me those dreams? What do you want from me and why me?"

Her eyes were wide now searching for anything on the valley floor. Her body ached as she continued to plead, "My Grandfather said this was a vision. I have traveled through pain along with others to get here. There must be something you have for me to learn." Still, nothing had changed.

Disbelief swept over her. She began to wonder if it was even a real vision now. "If this means something, you must tell me. I just need to know." The silence continued as she looked towards an Indian paintbrush flower. "Anything. Just tell me anything," she pleaded. "What is it you want me to do?" This was the first time that the solitude was unsettling for her. Frustration, fear, and confusion were gradually building inside of her until she finally shed a single tear trickling down her face.

Hopeless, she couldn't bear to be there anymore. She finally got up since there were no signs. She kept repeating those requests to herself on the way down the ridge tormenting herself. Making her way back towards the lucid lake she wondered if she would sleep at all tonight even though she was drained. She was sure her mind wouldn't be able to stop. She wiped away her tears as she saw that Wandering Bear and Swift Runner had made a small fire.

Chapter Six

Once she made it back to the campsite, Swift
Runner asked, "Did anything happen? Did you see any..?"
She stopped her questions when she saw the
disappointment on Morning Flower's face.

Morning Flower shook her head, "I think I am
going to get some rest now."

Her friend insisted, "Here, Wandering Bear caught
some fish and cooked some. You should eat a little before
you sleep. I made some Wakinakim poultice and tea to help
with your arm. How is it feeling?"

"Umm, it is alright. I have had too much on my
mind to notice," answered Morning Flower.

Swift Runner reached out handing her the tea, as she took a sip its warmth began to trickle inside her. With the crisp nightly air coming, Morning Flower untied her pack and wrapped herself in her bison hide. She sat silently by the crackling fire, eating the trout.

Wandering Bear and Swift Runner could tell that she was upset and looked at each other trying to figure out how to comfort her.

Morning Flower's human companions weren't the only ones to notice the change in her emotions. Leaping Ears had heard Morning Flower's voice and uncurled herself from her nap to lay next to her. Nina stood and limped over to Wandering Bear, laying on the other side of him. Red Storm continued to graze close by as the screech owls were trying to find worms on the lake's muddy beach.

Morning Flower was so hungry that she ate two fish by herself, except for the small portions she gave to the fox and wolf. While she ate, Swift Runner unwrapped her arm and applied the poultice. The wound stung at first, but the plaster began to relieve some of the throbbing.

Morning Flower was beginning to feel uncomfortable with all eyes set on her. "I was thinking of calling the girl owl Bright Eyes and the boy owl Mighty Beak. What do you think?" she asked trying to break some attention off of herself.

"Those names fit perfectly," Swift Runner agreed.

Wandering Bear let out a gentle laugh, "They really do."

Morning Flower could tell they wanted to know more about how the hike up the ridge went, but the sting of the unanswered questions was still fresh and she didn't feel like talking about it right then. "Thanks for the fish and tea, but I think I should rest now. I feel like I have been up for many moons," sighed Morning Flower. Before they could respond she turned away so her back was towards the fire and curled up in her blanket. Red Storm came over and laid down beside her. Leaping Ears' tail swished over Morning Flower's face as the fox turned in a circle to lay near the girl's head. Just as she thought, she was drained but her mind was too busy to fall asleep quite yet.

What am I going to tell Grandfather when we go home? Am I supposed to stay on the mountain until the Great Spirit reveals an answer? Was I supposed to have gone on the trip alone with no help to find out the truth behind the dream? Her mind began to feel clogged as the questions kept coming and coming. There seemed to be no answers to aid her. Then her mind was distracted by the conversation around the campfire. She tried to be still as the discussion began.

When Swift Runner thought that Morning Flower was asleep she spoke quietly, "What do you think happened up there?"

Wandering Bear was drawing with one of the cooled charred sticks in the dirt. He stopped and looked

118

towards the ridge that Morning Flower had come back from as he answered, "I am not sure. Maybe she did not like the answer she got."

"I wish she would have told us. Maybe we could have helped," she sighed. She had never had her closest friend not share something with her. She truly didn't know what else to do for her.

"I think this something she has to do herself. I think we have done what we can for now, but I know what you mean. I feel kind of helpless." He tried to reassure her as he returned to drawing with his stick.

Swift Runner bit her lip because she was hesitant to speak again, but decided it was her turn to open up. She readjusted and sat on her knees before she spoke up. "You know Morning Flower is my best friend. She has always been there for me. We have always been together, but we really became best friends when my dad died." She paused,

"She was the first person to see me crying over him. I remember sitting by a tree, not knowing she was in the tree, when she climbed down from it and just hugged me. She did not say anything, just hugged me. Ever since then we have been together like moss on a rock. I have never seen her talk to someone new as much as she does with you. She does not really talk about herself or at all if she has too." Swift Runner exhaled as if she had been holding back all day to say that to him.

Wandering Bear drew his attention back to the young girl and questioned, "Why not? Is that why that boy called her Mouse?"

"Yes. Do you remember when we were younger and the tribe was still traveling? It was before we reached Awenasa, our home." asked Swift Runner.

"Yes but that was a while ago. That is when my family joined the tribe. What happened?" inquired Wandering Bear.

"Remember when we had crossed paths with another tribe. We tried to trade items before our next stop and some of their tribe members tried to capture some of our people while the others were busy. Morning Flower was one of them. Morning Flower's grandmother saw this, grabbed her granddaughter from the snatcher's hands and shouted to the Chief of the other tribe saying, 'We are making trades only for food and clothing. Not for children and if that is what you plan on doing there was to be no deal.' Our tribe has always had high respect for the Elders and what they say, so they believed her."

"Before she could continue, one of the other tribe's warriors killed her. A small war broke out. We won the war and they did not bother us again. As we buried our dead, Morning Flower's mother later told me that she had heard her daughter whisper to the Great Spirit that she would never stand up for herself as her grandmother had done. So her mother told me to keep an eye on her after she trusted me."

"That is why I was protective of her with you. I knew she would not stand up for herself. I now see how she wants me to be friends with you, so I will try. I guess you have been a little help so far. But if you ever hurt her," her eyes began to pierce his. "I will hunt you down and so will many others. She has many in her family and as you know they are not all people." She nodded her head towards the animals that surrounded them.

He looked in her direction and promised, "I will never hurt her."

She lightened her tone, "I know. You look at her the same way Nina and the other animals do. Your eyes soften, almost in the same way the owls look at each other." Swift

Runner raised one eyebrow jokingly questioning him. She looked at him expecting an answer or an explanation.

Instead, he rose up from his spot, wiped the soot off his hands and replied, "That is enough talk for one night. We should all get some rest. I am going to take a quick walk around the area to make sure that there are no signs of any predators. I can keep watch on the fire for a while too. Rest well Swift Runner," not waiting for her reply he walked away from the fire's light and was soon consumed by darkness.

Swift Runner chuckled to herself as she got ready for a good night of rest. She glanced at her friend once more hoping maybe there was a chance that she would turn around and open up to her about what had happened. Then again, she was glad she was able to talk to the boy and get that warning off her chest.

Morning Flower was glad her back was towards them because she didn't know how to take in all she had heard them talk about. From talking about her grandmother, herself, and now his eyes. She blushed slightly. *What was that all about?* She hadn't noticed anything, but now she was discovering that people had observed more about her than she meant.

She couldn't believe all that Swift Runner had told Wandering Bear. Not that she minded too much, after today's adventures she was beginning to trust him more. Then again, about what her mother had told Swift Runner too. Swift Runner had never told her those things. She didn't know her mother had heard her prayers that day. How had people noticed so much about her even when she was so careful not to reveal too much about parts of her own story to others?

Feeling that she was being watched she lifted her eyes to find those big dark eyes of Red Storm watching over her. She gave a small scratch to Red Storm's chin and

he brushed his lips on her cheeks as if to give her a kiss.

With his whiskers tickling her face she tried not to laugh.

He rubbed his neck on her shoulder to get a better angle for

scratching. She felt safe with the animals she had been

surrounded by. Their silent peace comforted her and

relaxed her enough to forget her worries so she could

finally fall asleep.

Indian Paintbrushes, the mountain, and sunrise all

flashed before her once more. She saw the fire sweeping up

from the valley and it began to climb up the mountainside.

She began to panic as the flames danced around the

flowers. Then with a single spark touching a petal, one of

the wildflowers engulfed in flames. The fire didn't cease

with the one flower. It continued to consume everything in

its wake, up and onto the ridge. Morning Flower began to

toss and turn as the dream captured her. A blaze began to

find its way closer and closer to the very top, but before it could Morning Flower bolted upright.

She was sweating, even with the frigid air around her. Her breathing was racing and her head was spinning. It was almost as if she could feel the flames coming for her. She began to look around trying to make sure she didn't wake anyone. The fire near them was already dim and only the embers were glowing. The smell of the smoke began to make her unsure if it would suddenly grow and swallow her as it did in her dream. Or was the dream more of a nightmare now?

Red Storm must have gotten up sometime before. There was an empty space letting in a chilling breeze from where he had been laying earlier. The moon was high and showing that his silhouette was grazing not far away. Morning Flower got up, trying not to bother Leaping Ears too much. She went over to the horse and wrapped her arms around his neck giving him a hug, trying to comfort herself.

126

He pushed her aside slightly as he bent his neck and began to forage once again.

Knowing the bottomless stomach of his was his main priority right now; she sat on the ground and looked into the never-ending night sky. The stars seem to twinkle back at her. She took a deep breath as she noticed how clear the heavens were that night. She loved how the night sky had such a depth to it that if she could reach out far enough maybe she could swim with the stars.

As she gazed at the reflection of the moon on the water from the lake everything on the mountain seemed to be still. How could she have had a nightmare up here with such peacefulness? Even the forest around the lake was silent. No animals were stirring or calling out to one another. She almost forgot what had awakened her.

Suddenly she heard footsteps coming towards her. It was Wandering Bear. They had never had a chance to talk alone since yesterday's collision. Since then so much had happened. Trying to be nonchalant, she continued to stay seated while he made his way over.

He sat down beside her and asked, "I woke up to check on the fire and noticed you were up. Could you not sleep?"

Remembering what she had overheard Swift Runner say earlier that night she answered him back with a simple shake of her head. She continued to look forward at the calm lake and the midnight sky's reflection on the water.

He remained quiet for a little while. He noticed that she had seemed distant but thought it might have been more about her quest not going as she might have wanted it to go. So he just sat next to her trying to figure out what to say next.

Without knowing why she began to speak, "Swift Runner was wrong you know." Morning Flower said with her face solemn.

Caught off guard by the statement he asked, "What do you mean?"

She stared at the water as ripples began to form on the lake. She continued, "I heard her tell you about my grandmother and the war. We did not win that fight. Nobody wins a battle."

He understood now what she was talking about. "I know. There is much pain on both sides of a war."

Her eyes followed a long-necked crane that was floating across the lake as she spoke, "I know she knows that too, but sometimes I think people forget that part of the war. Those who survive do not always feel the same way about battles."

Then, Wandering Bear became slightly embarrassed remembering the other details he had discussed with Swift Runner and wondered if she had heard that as well. Trying to get an understanding of how much she had heard he asked, "Are you upset that she told me about your grandmother?"

"No. I do not know. It is hard to say. I just..." she paused. "Even though I was young, I was close to my grandmother, and I have never told anyone about it." She noticed that she was beginning to talk more than she meant to and hushed herself.

"If you feel that I know you more than you know me now, I can tell you something I have not told anyone else," he sympathized. As she began to mull over what possible secrets he had, he began to explain. "I do not trust anyone that Nina does not like." He glanced back towards the passed out wolf as he continued, "A little bit after I helped her, she started getting used to my family and the

130

people in the village. But whenever my closest friend came around the fur on the back of her neck would rise and she would send a low warning growl. I just figured that she was jealous or still adjusting."

"Then one day I was out in the woods looking for her and I saw that my 'friend' had tied her to a tree and was throwing stones at her. She just sat there. She did not whine or howl. And she just... took it. I could not believe my so-called friend did that. Enraged I shouted at him demanding him to tell me what he was doing. He replied he was making her stronger. He tossed a jagged rock towards me as if he wanted me to join in. I tackled him to the ground and hit his face until Nina's rope broke free and she ran to me pulling my clothes trying to get us away from each other. During the wrestling, I accidentally elbowed her and I froze. She stopped pulling at me and sat. I told him never to come near us again or I would not stop next time. We have never spoken since. I sat with Nina and cleaned up the wounds from the rocks he tossed. Now if she does not get along with someone, I do not trust them either."

Wandering Bear was now the one looking off into the distance. Morning Flower glimpsed at him and the moonlight revealing the stern look on his face.

"That is why I trust you and Swift Runner. She adores you, which I think makes it even easier to trust you."

She didn't respond. How could she? She thought to herself. After a long pause, thinking she might have needed some more time to herself, Wandering Bear got up and started to walk away. Then he turned and said, "I almost forgot, I made this for your nightmares. I figured it might be why you were up so early yesterday. Hopefully, it will help you in case the Great Spirit does not reveal anything tonight." He pulled out a dreamcatcher. She looked at it as he handed it to her and she was in awe. "The feathers are from Mighty Beak and Bright Eyes. They kept cleaning each other, leaving feathers by the shore. So I thought you would like something to remember them by also."

As she held up the dreamcatcher in the moonlight the feathers dangled from the branched circle. She had not needed such a meaningful gift than she did tonight. As he turned to leave she whispered, "Thank you and I am sorry your friend hurt you and Nina. At least you have a few new friends now."

He let out a small smile, turned and went back to the fire, restocking it. Then he laid down beside the new warmth. Nina must have heard him stoke the fire. She waddled over towards him and lay by his side keeping him warm as he only had his summer breechcloth and leggings to wear.

Staring at the handmade dreamcatcher she wondered if it would help with tonight's sleep. She ran her fingers through the web and over the leather tassels. She stood up from her spot and pet Red Storm some more before she too returned to the fire. She snuggled in her blanket in an attempt to fall back asleep.

Leaping Ears hadn't moved since she got up, but Mighty Beak and Bright Eyes came over to join their protector. The two jumped up onto the tanned bison hide and began to huddle together. Morning Flower watched as Bright Eyes' face seemed to light up whenever she faced Mighty Beak. His face did the same as the little feathers on the top of his head began to twitch.

Morning Flower pet the top of Bright Eyes' head with her finger. She tried to pet Mighty Beak's head but he gave her a little snap with his beak. Luckily, the girl had faster reflexes. The two owls let out some short hoots before she tried to sleep again. She held the dreamcatcher with care and hoped that she would get some rest before tomorrow.

Before she knew it she awoke to Bright Eyes trying to burrow herself under the bison blanket. Mighty Beak was staring straight into Morning Flower's eyes. He tilted his head as he looked at her. Bright Eyes was now underneath the blanket and with a quiet hoot calling for Mighty Beak, he joined her. Morning Flower tried not to move as the two owls settled down near her stomach.

She realized that this was the first time in the past few days she had slept without any dreams or nightmares, whatever she was to call them. She saw that she was still holding the dreamcatcher that Wandering Bear had made her. Relieved that it had worked, she began to notice that the sky was starting to change into familiar colors. She felt like she had seen it somewhere before. Almost like in a dream. All of a sudden she had an idea.

She carefully got up trying not to bother the comfortable owls under the blanket. Attempting to make a cave for them she pushed the blankets together for the two. At first, Mighty Beak glared at her until he realized how cozy it was. He nuzzled closer to his love. Bright Eyes was humming with her eyes closed as she rested next to him.

Everyone else was sound asleep as Morning Flower cooed calling Red Storm and he trotted over to her. She tried to hop onto his back single handedly. After a few tries, she was successful and began to lead him towards the ridge where she was yesterday. With a slight nudge, she urged him to quicken his pace. As they made their way to the top of the mountain as the sky was starting to change into a shade of crimson pink. Once they reached a resting spot she hopped off Red Storm and began to pray as fast as possible. "Please, please, please show me something!" she begged.

She looked first at the flowers near her feet then across to the opposite mountain seeing if the sunlight had revealed anything. She remembered the next part of her vision and remembered the flames coming. She scanned the sides of the peak, afraid that they would become scorched if a fire began. She noticed off to the right something was odd. As she scanned the valley below, she became aware of the other village. She saw what she thought must have been one of their teepees was set on fire. "That must have something to do with the dream! Oh, thank you, thank you!" she dashed onto Red Storm once again and made her way towards her friends at their camp area.

Chapter Seven

As she arrived at the campsite she yelled, "Wake up! Wake up now! You have to come see this quick!!!" Startling the animals, they began to wake from their deep slumber. She shook Swift Runner and Wandering Bear until they awoke.

"What is happening?" said Swift Runner with a hint of grogginess.

"I do not know for sure but you have to come see. Something is wrong in the Cree village! Come on!" Morning Flower and Swift Runner jumped on the hefty horse while Wandering Bear did his best to sprint beside them.

As the group made it to the viewing point, Morning Flower pointed to where the teepee was ablaze, but something was different this time. She saw warriors were leaving the village. "Why would they leave and have the women stay with the teepee on fire?" Morning Flower asked.

After a brief pause, Wandering Bear uttered a groan, "They are going into battle! They have their weapons and their horses are painted, but where are they going?" he looked onward. Even from the mountaintop, it was easy to see some of the horses painted in bright blues and reds. "Oh no! Look what direction they are heading. The way they are traveling will take them down our valley and we are the only tribe nearby that I know of. It would take many more days to reach another tribe down the gorge. "

Fear had taken over Swift Runner's response, "But why would they go to war with us? We have been at peace for years. Maybe they are not going to our tribe."

Morning Flower began to look for their own tribe's hunting party. There was a large herd of bison that was on the prairie and she noticed some horses a little bit away from the herd. They must have been from her tribe.

"I do not know but we need to warn our tribe somehow and quick," Wandering Bear suggested, "Smoke signals?"

Morning Flower didn't want to risk another fire. She recommended, "We could try but we do not even know if they would be able to see it from the mountain. We would have to have a large enough fire for them to see, and with it being the dry season we would risk starting a fire that would grow wild. Then war and a fire might fall upon the village."

They eagerly made it back to the campsite to see what tools they had to start on a plan. Swift Runner was the first one to arrive, moving rapidly grabbing her water pouch and started fussing with her bison hide.

"What are you doing?" asked Wandering Bear.

"I have to go and tell the tribe. They need to know what is coming!" she exclaimed.

Morning Flower questioned her, "How are we all going to get there before the other tribe does? Especially with Nina's paw and we all cannot fit on Red Storm?"

Swift Runner finally stopped fussing over her moccasins and looked at Morning Flower replying, "You know why I have to do this and why I have to do this alone."

"No! You cannot..." Morning Flower stopped herself. She did know why Swift Runner had to go, but that didn't make it easier sending her by herself on such a risky trip.

Swift Runner whispering now, "This is my chance to be a scout and help someone else from being killed. Like... Like, my father. "

"Wait. What is happening?" the confused boy asked trying to get some answers.

But the two girls were already packing things up. "She has to run." Morning Flower responded.

"Can she take Red Storm?" he asked.

Swift Runner stopped rushing around and impatiently answered, "No, because he does not really listen to anyone but his girl," pointing her thumb towards Morning Flower. "And this is something I just have to do. By myself. Ok?"

"What if you get hurt or what if-?" Wandering Bear was cut off by Morning Flower as she held up her hand.

"No, she will be fine. Just stay on the trail so we can see your progress, but do not forget these." The older girl looked around until she found a maple tree seed. She reached for it and bent down next to Swift Runner tying the wing-shaped seed in her moccasin laces. As she stood up she smiled and said: "Run faster than the eagles soar."

Not expecting this response Swift Runner hugged Morning Flower. Morning Flower squeezed her back and encouraged her quietly, "You can do this. This is what you are meant to do. Now get going before another minute has passed. Do you have enough food?" She wiped a small tear away as she released her.

"I have some in my pouch, but if I get too warm running and leave my shawl on the trail could you pick it up for me? Mother will be mad if I lose it again." The girls laughed then grew quiet again.

"Be sure to be aware of your surroundings, okay? Remember the area where the mountain lion was and be extra cautious." Wandering Bear suggested.

Swift Runner nodded and began on her farewells. She patted Red Storm on the nose and looked at Nina, not even trying to pet her knowing Nina wouldn't allow it. The wolf appeared to smile as she panted. Leaping Ears tilted her head as she looked around. The owls were still in the cave made of blankets dosing. With another look and saying "See you back at the village," Swift Runner began her way on the trail they had come up on the day before. Her long flowing hair was seen darting between the pine trees down the path.

Wandering Bear began to wrap up Swift Runner's blanket and supplies while Morning Flower shooed the owls out of her own hide. Mighty Beak ruffled his feathers as he was disturbed from his cozy new home. The girl gently placed her dreamcatcher in her blanket hoping that her vision wouldn't come anymore and that whatever was going to happen ended peacefully. Once everything was packed up and Wandering Bear was sure the fire was put out, the two wasted no time gathering the animals and headed down the mountain.

Within minutes they were all set to go. Morning Flower was carrying the owls while Leaping Ears and Red Storm trotted behind her. Nina could walk almost completely by herself now but still had a slight limp.

Sooner than she had hoped, they made it to the area where they had first met Bright Eyes and Mighty Beak. Morning Flower stopped when she was sure they were close enough. She placed the owls on the ground and began to check on Bright Eyes' injured wing.

Mighty Beak seemed to get the idea once he looked around recognizing the area they were at. He placed his beak under hers nudging her. He began to flap his wings trying to encourage Bright Eyes to do the same. She tested out her wings and hopped around trying to see if the wing would be able to support her in flight. After a few tries, she made it off the ground. She took a low loop maneuvering around some trees and made her way back to her starting point. The two hooted in excitement and gave a last look towards Morning Flower before making their way through the forest.

"They will be alright." Wandering Bear reassured her.

She was glad she could help the feathery couple but was torn to see them go. She wished that maybe she could see them again, but right now she needed to get back on the trail and start her way home.

Down the trail, the group of five progressed at a quick pace. They found Swift Runner's shawl that she had left beside the trail. Morning Flower picked up the cloth and added it to her pack. With just Wandering Bear and herself with the ability to have a continuous conversation, she began to wish that one of their furry companions would suddenly have the Great Spirit give them a voice to help with the awkward silence that somehow seemed to fill the entire mountainside.

Though she usually didn't mind the silence, she felt for some reason she needed to break the stillness between them. Trying to quietly clear her throat she started, "The dreamcatcher helped. I was able to sleep well after you gave it to me." She gazed at her feet as they seemed to be speeding down the mountain.

"It did?" he was surprised.

She could tell that he was looking at her but she refused to look back. She nodded her head. Noticing her acting differently, Wandering Bear looked away from her.

To lighten the uncomfortable tension that seemed to continue to fill the air, Wandering Bear took a turn to ease the discomfort. Noticing Leaping Ears bounding ahead of them he asked, "So since I have met you, you have rescued a bison calf, helped with my wolf's paw, and saved an owl couple from possibly being eaten. You also helped a fox the day before. What are some of the other animals you have shared your gifts with?"

She reminisced for a moment before replying, "Well, I one time traveled by the river, down to the stream where the beavers are, and one of the beavers had his tail stuck under a tree so I lifted it off him. Another time a bat had flown onto a rock, also near the river, and the rock must have been wet because after it landed on the rock it slid into the river. So I helped the bat get out of the river

148

with a twig. And one time my brother had a skunk trapped in his teepee and I got it out."

"Did you get sprayed?" Wandering Bear laughed.

"I did not, but afterwards as a joke my brother tried to get the skunk to spray on me by scaring but the skunk sprayed him instead," she chuckled at the memory.

"You do have a way with the animals. I could not help but laugh a little when all the animals surrounded you as you slept last night. Do you remember the first time you helped an animal?" he inquired.

"My mother said that it started with a baby prairie dog when I was about my niece's age. She told me of how the baby prairie dog had been abandoned and that I tried to nurse it back to health. That is until my mother helped me find the other prairie dogs and we released the baby back to the family. "

"I do not know how you do it," he murmured. "I have only really helped out Nina and I love her so much. How are you able to let them go without missing them all?"

She sighed, "There are times when I do miss each of them and I am sad I have not seen some of them again. Other times I will see a few of them on my walks and they recognize me for a moment it seems and I know they are healthy and hopefully happy. Then we go our separate ways."

She looked at Leaping Ears, "I know Leaping Ears may not stay with me forever and will end up finding her own way in the wild. For now, I love that face, and it brightens my day when she hides behind a tree with only her ears sticking out. I want her to be happy, and right now she just seems happy to have an odd group for her pack."

At the sound of her name, Leaping Ears turned around and dashed back towards Morning Flower. Morning

Flower stopped walking for a moment to let the fox brush up against her leg and she pet her head.

Suddenly, Leaping Ears' head bolted up. With her fur frazzled, she began to look around. She let out a warning yelp and Nina began to join her with a definitive growl. Red Storms ears pinned back and he began to lean his weight on Morning Flower. Wandering Bear and Morning Flower followed the animal's actions and tried to spot the intruder.

Morning Flower noticed a nearby tree and saw familiar claw marks on it. Then a piercing scream was let out, but it wasn't from anyone in the group. They all began to search the dense forest looking for the one who gave out the cry.

Morning Flower thought she saw a tawny tail move from behind a bush. She blinked quickly hoping her eyes were playing tricks on her, but they weren't. As her eyes followed where the tail lead she saw the angry face of a large mountain lion prepared to pounce off of the branch it was resting on. Morning Flower couldn't decide if the tree was far enough away that the mountain lion couldn't jump on them or if she was underestimating the leap an angry wildcat could make.

Not wanting to find out she uttered, "What should we do?"

Wandering Bear didn't respond with words. He moved next to her, and then took another step forward to place himself between the wildcat and her. He stood tall with one of his fists clenched and the other placed on the knife on his side.

Nina had a wide stance and had naturally placed herself in front of the group. Leaping Ears stood behind Morning Flower peering out looking up towards the mountain lion. Red Storm was snorting at such a fast pace near Morning Flower's ear that it tickled. She wanted to move his head aside but was worried any movement would set off another shriek from the cat.

Everyone stared at the tree waiting for the cat's next move, as the mountain lion watched the group. Nina sent out a warning bark towards the predator. Not knowing whether that would help or not Wandering Bear tried to nudge her to stop, but Nina had started a riot. Red Storm began to bray loudly and stomp his hooves. While he clomped his feet a small dust cloud began to form. Leaping Ears began to feel courage forming and moved out from behind Morning Flower and let out her high pitched yap.

Morning Flower looked at Wandering Bear, shrugged and she began to whoop and holler. Wandering Bear joined after noticing the mountain lion's ears pinning further and further back. Red Storm then reared up and let his hooves go flailing in the air.

The mountain lion nearly fell out of the tree but quickly caught itself with its sharp claws. The outnumbered cat then jumped down and sped off in the other direction. Before long they could no longer see the mountain lion. Leaping Ears continued to bark as if to rejoice in the victory. Nina joined her with a chilling howl.

Wandering Bear said, "Maybe we should ride for a little while to get out of this area just in case the mountain lion would rather stalk its prey from behind."

Morning Flower agreed and tried to get on Red Storm on her own, but with her arm still sore from the previous day's wound she was struggling. Wandering Bear held out his clasped hands and she stepped on them helping her mount Red Storm. Morning Flower scooted forward so that Wandering Bear could easily hoist himself onto the horse's speckled rump.

With a sound of the mountain lion letting out an aggressive yowl in the distance the girl wasted no time nudging Red Storm with her knees to get him to trot quickly down the peak. Red Storm walked briskly with his head high as if he was satisfied that his rearing turned the frightful mountain lion into a racing scaredy cat.

Now that Morning Flower was able to relax, knowing that their life wasn't in danger of being in a fight with an enormous cat, she began to notice more of the smaller details of the trail. The sweet smell of the pine trees and, the sound of a woodpecker tapping a tree nearby. There was even a large moose who strode through some thickets off in the distance. She wanted to try and take her protective stallion around the mountain again on another trip, maybe one that was less time sensitive.

She also began to notice her empty stomach. She reached into her pouch and grasped for some food to offer Wandering Bear. As she reached for another handful for herself she touched the mysterious object she had found on the plains where the helpful boy joined the trip. She pulled it out and her mind began to mull over the forgotten object.

Wandering Bear looked over her shoulder curious about what she was looking at. "Maybe someone from the tribe will have seen it before?" he tried to reassure her.

She hoped his words were true and placed it back in her pouch, putting it out of her mind.

Luckily the downhill trek was going faster than yesterday's uphill excursion. Morning Flower could start to see their village in the distance as they were beginning to break through the trees and reach the valley. "Do you notice anything at the village yet?" she asked feeling anxious about what news there would be once they arrived.

"Not really. Soon we will be out of the tree line and it will be easier to see," he tried to put her at ease. After a few more turns down the path on the slope, they made it into the valley.

With a quick refill on everyone's energy and some long deserved drinks from the stream, they started back up again. The two continued to ride Red Storm and now that the village was closer his energy came like a second wind. Morning Flower egged him on even more. They tried to avoid the bison graveyard in case of another disaster. They could see no one on the horizon from where they were. No other people from their own tribe or from the neighboring village.

Morning Flower tried to stop asking Wandering Bear questions she knew he didn't know the answers to either. *Were their people in hiding? Had Swift Runner arrived in time to send out their own warriors? Would they fight the battle somewhere else or had they not been warriors at all? Instead was it just the elders coming to have a village gathering?* Morning Flower fearing the worst but prayed that it was the latter. *Surely if there was a war by now they would have heard battle cries. Right?*

She continued to encourage Red Storm to quicken his stride. Even with the two of them on his back and the long travels today and the day before he was already going at a surprisingly quick pace. Leaping Ears was not far behind them, but Nina was further back. Her paw was still sore but she continued forward, following the group as quickly as she could.

They were getting closer until Wandering Bear reaching around Morning Flower's arms and gently pulled the stallion's mane, bringing Red Storm to a halt. He slid off the horse's back and began to scan the fields for any sign from the village. Morning Flower tried to be patient as he did so. The break gave Leaping Ears and Nina a chance to catch up.

158

He checked Nina's paw as she sat panting with a tired grin. "Morning Flower, maybe you should wait here with the animals. Nina is still injured and Red Storm needs to rest. I do not want to send you into the village if there is trouble. I can go run and check if everything is alright then I will come back and get you."

"No! It was my dream that brought us up the mountain in the first place and I am the one who saw the other tribe heading over. Swift Runner has already left us to tell our people and I cannot wait around in a safe haven while everyone I know and love is at the risk of being hurt or worse. No, I am going with you!"

He noticed the worry on her face as she waited for his response. He knew that there was no way to make her stay, but he couldn't let her risk all of their health either.

Chapter Eight

A yellow-breasted meadow larch whistled as it flew past them in the field. Wandering Bear was about to answer but squinted to try and make a new discovery along the skyline to help object her points. She couldn't stand and wait for him to let her follow him. She scooted forward on her horse's back and intertwined Red Storm's mane with her fingers.

Noticing her preparation to ride on, the lean boy sped in front of the horse holding his arms up, "Okay, okay. You can come." He placed one hand gently on Red Storm's chest keeping him in place. "But if there is any sign of trouble you have to leave. No questions," his face was stern while he spoke.

"No, we all will leave," she answered but her face reflected his firm expressions.

He walked beside them as they continued their way to the far side of the village. They agreed that it would be better to go in calmly since they still couldn't pick up on any signs of stirring in the village.

As they got closer everything seemed to be unusually quiet. Wandering Bear peeked his head in one of the nearby teepees but just like the rest of the village, it was empty. All of their senses were on high alert waiting for something to unfold and give them an idea of what had happened to their entire tribe.

"Maybe they went to the cave on the hill. We have never had to use it as a safe place before but we have never needed to either. Even the horses are gone. Let us head that way first. If they are not there it will give us a better point

of view for which way they could have gone," Wandering
Bear suggested.

Morning Flower tried to look at any fresh tracks
while up on Red Storm but being so close to the village it
made it hard to tell. The village was a well traveled area
which made it was difficult to separate the old tracks from
the new ones. Once they were out of the community she
noticed that some of the horse prints had split off towards
the valley while the others continued up the hill. With this
hint, they quickened their pace again.

Red Storm could sense the urgency and didn't stop
for any grazing moments. Leaping Ears didn't wander
ahead as her curious self usually did. She stayed close to
Nina's side. While Nina limped, the two were panting.
They were grateful when they finally arrived at the cave
and no longer had to guess what to do next.

The exhausted boy and girl were relieved when they found almost the entire tribe was inside the deep cave. Most of the clan's members were sitting while a few others were on their knees trying to see who was coming from the outside of the cave. Morning Flower nearly fell off of Red Storm as she looked around trying to find someone from her family.

Finally, her mother came rushing over, grabbing her daughter down from the horse and hugging her. "I was so worried that you would be caught in the middle of... What happened to your arm and dress? You are covered in blood! And why am I not surprised to see a fox following you? Are you hurt?" Spring Frost continued to look between Morning Flower, Leaping Ears, and the slightly familiar wolf. Then she noticed Wandering Bear, who seemed to be waiting nearby them. He continued to watch the encounter between the mother and daughter as he stood by the stallion.

"I am alright Mother," Morning Flower tried to answer but her mother didn't let her continue.

Spring Frost began with the questions again but this time asking the strange boy who was near her, "What do you want?" her mother seemed to hug Morning Flower with a protective motive this time.

Morning Flower explained, "That is Wandering Bear. He helped Swift Runner and me on our trek to Eagle Mountain."

Before Wandering Bear could say hello Spring Frost jumped in, "Do not get me started on that little trip! Your Grandfather told me about that and you did not even leave without a goodbye," her mother's face came across as hurt.

"I kissed your forehead," she confessed. "Did Grandfather explain why he thought I should go? Where is he?" Morning Flower asked looking around for him to help aid her against her mother's interrogation.

"Yes," her mother replied solemnly. "And I will admit it was a good reason you went. I think he went for a walk. Swift Runner returned in time for us to gather some items and come to the caves. We were able to send another runner to send a message to the hunters on the bison raid, but that is all we know of so far."

"They did not send Swift Runner to warn the bison raid, did they?" worried Morning Flower.

"No, she is over by her mother resting. She said she left at sunrise, but she got here before the high sun. She must have ran so fast. I am surprised she was able to walk once she arrived. As soon as her mother reassured her that everything was going to be alright, she laid her down and the girl fell fast asleep. Let her rest for now," Spring Frost told her knowing her daughter, who began to fidget to find her exhausted friend and would wake her if she could.

Morning Flower could see Swift Runner towards the middle of the cave asleep on her mother's lap, who was brushing Swift Runner's hair out of her face. Her little sister, Moonbeam, was with them but her brother was not. Swift Runner's mother, Falling Leaf, must have let him go on the hunt. That must be what the additional look of worry on her face was for.

Morning Flower began to look more into the cave. She noticed the people from her tribe from a different view. They all seemed frightened. She had only seen that many of the tribe afraid a few times before. She didn't like the feelings that were coming to her as she looked at the gloom on their faces.

She saw her sister-in-law, Wild Dove, embracing Little Duck in her arms as if she would never let her go.

166

Small Chief was trying to be brave for his own mother by sitting with his legs crossed and arms folded. He also had rubbed dirt on his face the way the warriors would and it seemed to bring Golden Aspen a small smile that too quickly vanished. Some were praying, while others sat stone-faced, quiet and giving a blank stare.

Leaping Ears sat at Morning Flower's feet trying to not be noticed by anyone. Since they were standing near the entrance of the cave Red Storm stretched his head to reach for some all too delicious grass that he had been longing for. The girl noticed some of the horses were hiding in the thicket of trees near the entrance. Only the young foals didn't seem to know that there might be a danger heading their way. One of the young paints tried to chase a butterfly before an older horse butted his nose on the foals' side to make it stop.

Morning Flower snapped out of her observations when her mother asked her, "What all happened during your trip? Swift Runner only told the details needed for us to decide what needed to be done quickly. Come here let me look at your wound." She eagerly ushered Morning Flower and even Wandering Bear to sit in order to hear her daughter tell her tale. Leaping Ears curled up in Morning Flower's lap and the exhausted Nina rested her head on Wandering Bear's lap.

Once they settled in she told her mother of the journey. How Wandering Bear and Nina had joined them after the bison calf injured her, helping Bright Eyes and Mighty Beak, the top of the mountain, seeing the teepee on fire and even the mountain lion.

She left out the part of how she overheard Swift Runner talking about how her mother had asked her friend to stand up for Morning Flower. Since she was unsure how she felt about the matter and didn't want to bring up the sad subject of her grandmother's passing again, especially since it had come up a few times too many for her comfort in the

168

past few days. She also didn't talk of the dreamcatcher, she wasn't sure why she left out this part but she glanced at Wandering Bear and realized she was, for some reason, slightly embarrassed about receiving such a personal and much needed gift at that moment.

Her mother listened quietly while Morning Flower talked, waiting until the end to speak. "That is truly incredible." She sat speechless just gazing at the group before her.

Once again, not thrilled by the attention she was beginning to receive; Morning Flower lifted Leaping Ears off her lap and placed her to the side. Morning Flower stood up and walked over to Red Storm and began to scratch his belly. "You did great today," she whispered in his ear.

She tried to avoid eye contact with anyone and continued rubbing under his chin. Since he was so tired, instead of his usual lip quivering he leaned his neck on her. The weight of his neck caught her off balance. With this distraction, she was unable to overhear Spring Frost thanking Wandering Bear for his willingness to stay with her daughter and protect her. She also missed Wandering Bear's reply that she was more than capable of taking care of herself.

Morning Flower could feel her own energy begin to drain as she sat beside Red Storm as he nibbled on the grass around him. She laid her arms on the horses back and rested her head on her arms. If it weren't for all of the uneasiness of the situation she would have fallen asleep, but there was too many thoughts on her mind. She paid no attention to the conversations going on behind her. She looked over Red Storm's back and tried to see if she could spot anything in the valley. Now it would be the dreadful wait for any sign of an attack.

Now that she wasn't busy running around, the pain of her arm began to set in. She readjusted her sitting position and loosened her bandage. Leaping Ears came and tried to dip her nose into Morning Flower's pouch. Morning Flower tried to shoo her away then realized how hungry she was herself. She gave some food to the starving fox and then herself. While she was handing Leaping Ears some jerky her bandage began to slip off her arm and revealed the size of the wound that was underneath.

Her mother happened to look at her just then. Without a word she came over and began to look over Morning Flower's arm. A look of sorrow came across Spring Frost's face. Spring Frost gently touched the gash on Morning Flower's upper arm. Morning Flower tried not to wince as her mother placed her fingers near the injury.

Her mother held back her feelings and grabbed the waterskin, she wetted down some of the bandages and began to clean the wound. It had slowly started to heal but at least there was no sign of infection. It might have helped if the wound was cleaned once she woke today but there was no time.

Now that the bandages were dirty Spring Frost set them aside and tore off a thicker piece of a tassel from her dress and began to wrap Morning Flower's arm. Morning Flower's jaw dropped. Her mother had always gotten upset when she had come home with another self-made tear in her own dress but now she just had done the same.

"Why did you do that mother?" she stuttered.

"I now know why you do it yourself." She veered her eyes towards Nina as she lay next to Wandering Bear licking her paw. She continued, "In the moment you think of nothing else but to help whoever is in need. You do it almost to offer a part of yourself to aid them. I just wanted to do the same for you. Wandering Bear told me more about how you helped those animals. You did not tell the

172

story the way he did. Even though you thought you were in a race with the sun to know about your vision, you took the time to help those who needed instead of passing by and continuing on your path." She had finished wrapping her daughter's arm and leaned to kiss her forehead. "I am so proud of you," she whispered and this time she knew that Morning Flower heard her.

Chapter Nine

Her mother rose, leaving her to rest. Leaping Ears was already fast asleep on Morning Flower's lap once again. Morning Flower stroked the soft bright copper colored fur while closing her eyes to get a quick nap. She was now resting her head on Red Storm's comfortable plump stomach and the small amount of noise from inside the safe shelter began to fade away. Her body had a slight ache but she was sure that Swift Runner was much sorer and she would hear about it soon. She was so relaxed her body gave a slight twitch as she drifted to sleep.

Not long after dozing off, she was awoken by the ground quaking. Red Storm stood up and with this motion Morning Flower's head slid off of him. She looked around and saw the hunters of her tribe trudging up the hill. Everyone within the cavern began to stir again and flocked to the mouth of the cave. Since Morning Flower wasn't there to see the send-off she wasn't sure who had come back and who had not returned. She knew that even if the hunt had gone well, there was most likely going to be no supplies from the bison raid.

She tried to look for her father and brother's horses but with the crowd all searching for their own loved ones it made it hard to spot them. She smiled and waved as she finally saw her father on his horse, Gliding Feather. Her heart sank as the familiar horse next to him was her brother's, Sundance, and the horse was barebacked. She quickly turned to face her mother. Spring Frost saw that Sundance was without a rider and raced to Wild Dove and Little Duck. Spring Frost began to support her when her daughter-in-law saw no immediate signs of him.

Morning Flower noticed that her father's horse was pulling a travois. A small ray of hope returned to her. The women of her family squeezed through the crowd and made their way towards Tall Oak. He was covered in a mixture of blood and mud. She hoped that the blood was from the hunt and nothing more. He comforted them as he began to explain what had happened to his son. He got off Gliding Feather and showed them Cloud Jumper was on the wooden frame behind the horse.

Her brother lay still grasping at his leg where an arrow had struck its mark. Wild Dove tossed Little Duck into Morning Flower's arms and bent to Cloud Jumper's side. She kissed his cheeks while he brushed her untamed hair out of his face.

He winced when his mother touched the skin around the arrow. She trembled holding back her tears, "Now I have two children with injuries. What am I to do with you two?"

Her family turned to see what Morning Flower's injury had been but she tried to move Little Duck in a way that it would cover most of her bandaged arm. Her mother began to tend to Cloud Jumper's leg as her father began to ask what had happened but Morning Flower interrupted and asked the question first, "What happened?"

He grunted, "We began our hunt yesterday after being delayed because Grandfather had to explain to us why you and Swift Runner had seemed to vanish. Which we will talk about later," he muttered.

He gave a stern look towards Morning Flower but her warm eyes encouraged him to continue with the story. "The hunt went well. We had killed a few good sized bison that would have been good for the clan. But Kicking Bird had run to tell us just moments before about what Swift Runner had said about our neighboring clan. We tried to prepare ourselves hoping we would not come to a fight but they surprised us and came from a different direction than we thought they would. We had almost the same amount of warriors as them but we were already tired from the hunt. Luckily the fighting spirit came to us all. Both sides fought hard but we had to withdraw from the fight because too many were hurt and killed. We were grateful that they did not continue the battle and follow us. They turned and headed back to their own village."

Some women from the tribe began to wail at the tragic news that their loved ones would not come home. Morning Flower looked around the cave. She saw the despair in not only the faces of the women who had lost someone but in the men who had told them. A great pain had struck the hearts of her people. She was glad to have Cloud Jumper return with only a minor injury compared to others but felt guilty of her own happiness. She could sense that the warriors had also a hint of remorse, as they had survived when their friends had not.

Many women and Elders helped the warriors get more comfortable and began to provide aid to their wounds. So much blood was on the men as well as the horses. Red Storm pinned his ears back as he was sniffing the blood on Gliding Feather. Morning Flower was still holding her niece trying to distract the toddler from her father's injuries. She stayed out of the way and stood near the trees.

Leaping Ears was hiding behind her staying as close as possible, hoping no one would shoo her away or harm her, but everyone was too upset to notice the small fox.

Morning Flower looked around and saw that Swift Runner's brother had found his family. Swift Runner was still sound asleep as Falling Leaf placed her head carefully on the cave floor and hugged her son. Morning Flower was glad that she would not have to comfort her friend again, as she had when Swift Runner's father passed.

After a few minutes of the clan's arrival, some of the warriors began to become enraged as they told of what had happened. One warrior named Fire Maker pushed aside the help of an Elder and began to shout, "We must go and fight back! They took many lives and we must fight to protect ourselves from looking weak!"

A shorter woman by the name of Autumn Sun replied in agreement, "Yes and you must bring back my son so we can bury him."

Morning Flower began to see the anger spread through the clan quickly. Spring Frost turned to her husband and pleaded, "What about Dancing Star? What if our tribe does attack their village? She might get hurt. If there is a war you must try and stop it, Tall Oak!"

His face grew grim, "I did not see Fighting Bull during the battle. Maybe he stayed with her and will be able to protect her."

She wouldn't stand for it, though, "No! If there is another battle it must be stopped. Two of our children have already gotten hurt enough I cannot have another one brought to harm!"

Tall Oak saw the sorrow in Spring Frost's eyes and went over to the Chief, Brave Tomahawk. Morning Flower tried to read his lips but there was too much commotion going on around them to make out anything.

The Chief spoke loud enough to talk over the commotion, "Enough blood is on the valley floor today. We will rest for tonight and leave at dawn in two groups. One group will go with us and return with our lost warriors. The other will continue to our neighbors' village and try to talk about why the fight took place. If they do not want to tell us why they fought we will be prepared to fight." He looked at her father, who seemed not to agree with the Chief's decision fully, but nodded his head with respect.

The tribe began to move slowly out of the cave and down towards their homes. Some warriors cleaned the blood off themselves while others like Fire Maker refused to wash and kept themselves filthy. They did this to show the other tribe of the blood that was shed today. There were no stories shared around a campfire tonight. Not even of how well the hunt had gone since it would only remind them of the battle that happened afterward.

With her family busy taking care of her brother Morning Flower tried to make herself useful. She took Gliding Feather, Sundance and Red Storm near the stream and began to wash the horses. She brought Little Duck along as well to distract her from the toddler's father's pain. Leaping Ears slowly became her joyful self as they furthered themselves from the angry crowd and reached the stream. Morning Flower placed her niece near the stream. The toddler sat quietly until the fox bounced near her and kept her entertained.

As Morning Flower started to wash the blood off of the light golden appaloosa she heard footsteps behind her. She turned her head to see Nina and Leaping Ears greeting each other like old friends and Wandering Bear was not far behind them.

He noticed the small girl by the stream and asked Morning Flower, "How are your brother and father doing? I thought I saw your brother with an arrow in his leg," he tried to whisper the last part, trying not to alarm the little one.

"They are alright, better than most. Cloud Jumper got the worst of it out of the two, though." She was about to ask about his own family then realized she didn't know much about his family. "How is your family handling this?" she was trying to be broad with her question.

"My dad and brothers are alright. A few cuts here and there, but that is pretty usual for them," he began to clean the mud off of Red Storm from their own two-day travels.

"How many brothers do you have?" she asked as she plucked a mud clot off of the mare's hindquarters.

"I have three older brothers; Hunting Moose, Eagle Eye, and Long Knife. They all went on the hunt and did not believe me when I told them that we faced a mountain lion head on." he laughed.

Morning Flower smiled and wondered what else she didn't know about him.

"Have you seen Swift Runner yet?" he asked not intentionally changing the subject.

"I saw her but she was still sleeping. She is probably so tired that she will sleep for another whole day."

Sundance couldn't wait for his own bath and dipped himself in the stream.

184

Wandering Bear replied, "I cannot believe that she made it down so quickly."

"I can. She runs every day," she reminded him.

Morning Flower noticed that Gliding Feather's fur began to clear up but the water began to grow dingy. As her mind turned to a more serious note, she asked, "What do you think is going to happen tomorrow?"

He continued to scrub an extra tough spot on Red Storm's flank as he paused and chose his words with care, "I do not know. I think it is risky but I also know that many will not settle until something is sorted out."

Little Duck let out a cheerful laugh as Leaping Ears was trying to get Nina to play with her but Nina sat still, brushing the eager fox away. The two teens continued to clean the horses but in silence thinking about what possibilities would happen tomorrow. Once the horses were as clean as they needed to be for tonight, Wandering Bear and Morning Flower stopped washing them.

Red Storm trotted over and rolled in a dirt pile. Covering his clean self and returned to his more natural state. Gliding Feather snorted at her colt with disapproval. Morning Flower and Wandering Bear left the horses to graze while the fox and wolf followed close behind. They went their own ways and the girl, the toddler and Leaping Ears made it back to check on their family.

She found them outside of Cloud Jumper and Wild Dove's teepee surrounding her brother and mending him. Grandfather was there though and it was the first time that she had seen him since the beginning of her own adventure. Grandfather seemed to be unsure whether this was the right time to ask for all the details of how her journey went. The rest of the family had their mind too occupied, they didn't even notice the fox was still trailing her around. She sat still with Little Duck on her lap and patted the top of the fox's head while listening to her family talk.

"No, Cloud Jumper. You will stay! You cannot even walk and Wild Dove would not be able to handle you going in this condition," stated her father. "Besides the Chief said that we will only be bringing a few people to gather our fallen warriors. If you cannot walk you would have to return with them anyway."

Wild Dove grabbed Cloud Jumper's face towards her own, "They will be fine. You are staying right here until you are healed completely. No more talking about it. It is final." After she had finished her statement she continued to help with his wound and that was the end of the fight from him.

Morning Flower grinned. She always loved to see Wild Dove and her mother be so gentle but then when it came to the safety of their families they stood their ground and wouldn't let it be any other way.

Grandfather finally made his way over towards his granddaughter. She remembered the object she had found the day before and trying not to stir her drowsy niece maneuvered her one free hand to reach into her pouch and grab it. "Have you seen this before Grandfather? I thought if anyone had seen something that is new to me, you might know what it would be."

Grandfather looked over the tiny dense rock and held it up to get a better look at it. "Sorry little one, I have not. Did you find that along your travels?"

She nodded her head as she put it away, a little discouraged as to still not know what it could be.

Her Grandfather noticed her downcast face. "Looks as if you did good kid," he patted her back as she looked at him. "It could have been a lot worse if you did not go searching for answers." They watched as her mother and sister-in-law fussed over her brother.

"Thanks for the push Grandfather, otherwise I do not think I would have gone."

He gave a slim smile as he replied, "Do you know why I told the story at the campfire the other night?"

Morning Flower shook her head as she rocked Little Duck to sleep.

"I just felt like I should. I did not want to at first, but I remembered it being one of your Grandmother's favorites and just had a feeling deep down that it was time to share it. Sometimes there are going to be things in life when you do not want to do something but you know you need to. Do you understand?"

Morning Flower thought about his words. She understood but she wasn't sure if she would always take up the courage to do what needed to be done.

The village seemed to be restless that night. Morning Flower continued to ponder as she looked around the clan and saw many people trying to keep themselves busy. Only a few of the warriors who had been injured had managed to fall asleep. With the endless possibilities of how tomorrow would go, no one seemed to risk sleep to quicken the night.

Some of the women who had lost a son or husband cut their hair in grief. While others held out the hope, staring off into the darkened valley that since they had not seen their loved ones pass away there was a miracle that they had survived not only the battle but the night as well. Some of the younger children didn't seem to understand why their mothers or grandmothers were wailing and with confusion cried along with them. Morning Flower was

190

worried it was going to be a long night and an even longer day for those who will be waiting for the news of the conflict.

It was late at night before Morning Flower began to feel the wave of the past two days events wash over her. She made her way back to her own teepee. While she was unpacking her things from her journey the dreamcatcher fell out of her pouch. As she covered herself with her blanket, she held the dreamcatcher. She watched Leaping Ears use her nose to open the flap of the teepee and sneak over to where she was laying. The sneaky fox rested her body near Morning Flower, making sure that she was hidden if someone were to come in. With a sweet lick on Morning Flowers chin, Leaping Ears turned and went to sleep within seconds. Not long afterward Morning Flower joined the fox in slumber.

> > > > >

A wave of flames continued to burn the colorful wild Indian paintbrush flowers. The wind swirled the flames, creating a larger gust of heat, scorching the leaves and grass. Just as there seemed to be no hope and the flames would consume everything in its path everything was brought to a halt. The first paintbrush flower that Morning Flower had seen in her first dreams stood alone on the top of a peak.

Then a curious thing happened. The red flower began to shine brighter and brighter until it was nearly as bright as the sun itself. With that, the flames died down and even the embers of the fire showed no color. As the fire ceased, the damage of what it had done was revealed. Most of the mountainside was now charred and lifeless. A slight breeze scattered ashes down to the valley. The flowers that were untouched swayed in the light wind and their seeds began to fall onto the darkened soil. Suddenly a soft rain fell and the grass and seeds began to sprout. Peace seemed to have returned and there was now more flowers than there

had been before the fire.

Chapter Ten

With the clatter of something falling outside the teepee, Morning Flower was wide awake. As she looked around for the culprit of the noise she saw her mother was still asleep but not her father. The place where he would usually lay was left empty. After her dream, she was once again unsure what it had all meant. Surely the dreams would have stopped once she had seen the warriors heading towards her village and Swift Runner warned them of the chance of a battle. *But why would I still be having the same dream?*

It struck her. *I must go with my father on the trip today. Maybe there was something more that was happening and it would fall into place along the way.* With no time to waste she jumped up, alarming the dozing fox and sped outside to find her father. Tall Oak was bent over picking up his arrows that had fallen out of his quiver.

"I need to go with you today," whispered Morning Flower behind him.

Startled, Tall Oak nearly dropped the arrows again. He replied, "It is too dangerous. You must not come with me today." He pointed to her arm and continued, "You still need to heal. You need to help your mother and take care of Wild Dove, Cloud Jumper, and Little Duck. You are needed here."

Morning Flower was never one who would argue but she was sure that there was something going to happen that she needed to know on the trip. "You do not understand. I keep having this vision and for a little bit it stopped, but once I found out about the trip it came back again last night with a different ending. I need to know what it means. The dream helped us warn you and the others about the battle. It must mean something else is coming, but I will not know if I do not come with you. Besides, it will save someone from having to run and warn our people about something again."

Tall Oak was surprised. He hadn't heard her talk so much to him in a long time, especially with that passion. He paused for a moment looking her over as if waiting for her to change her mind, but she stood firm, trying to hold her ground like her mother would. He sighed, "Well if you are to come I can hear more about this trek of yours that your grandfather was so sure about. As soon as we arrive where the warriors lay you *will* go back with the group returning home. Understood?"

She continued to put up a fight as she fidgeted with the tassels on her dress, "Then I will separate from the group and continue trailing you. The Great Spirit is giving me these dreams and I must find out what they mean."

196

Tall Oak recognized defeat when he saw it. "Any sign of trouble though and you will come back to Awenasa."

She agreed but was unsure whether she would keep that promise.

It was dawn now and the others from the tribe began to prepare themselves once again. They packed lighter since there would be a possibility of battle. Some of the other men, such as Fire Maker, painted arrows on their horse's hooves for speed and fire arrows on the horse's front shoulders for strength. The Chief and Tall Oak were some of the few who did not paint their horses with hopes of revenge against the other clan.

Morning Flower was looking around for Swift Runner when she felt her braids being tugged from behind. As she spun around she saw the tired face of her best friend and embraced her. "I heard of how fast you made it back. Nice running!" congratulated Morning Flower.

Swift Runner glanced down at Morning Flower's pack and asked, "You seem to be going with them?"

Morning Flower gave her a brief update on her dream and why she planned to join them. Swift Runner's smile dropped. "I would go with you but my little sister told me of how mother cried while I was gone and Crazy Legs was on the raid. I think it would be too soon for me to leave her again. She can not stop him from going but I can not put her through that worry again. Will you be okay?"

Morning Flower saw Falling Leaf's face in the crowd as she hugged Crazy Legs one more time as if she could barely stand to let her boy go. Her eyes were red from all the crying and her cheeks were tear stained. "I understand. My father will be there. I think she needs you more right now."

"Well do not have too many adventures without me," she teased and hugged Morning Flower again before helping her friend mount the stallion. She patted Red Storm on the rump and told him, "You run quickly if she's in trouble. Alright, Red Storm?" He snorted in return and Swift Runner made her way back to her family with her sore stiff legs barely being able to take her there.

Only a few women would be accompanying them on the journey to retrieve the warriors who had passed away and to see if they could scavenge anything from the bison raid. Spring Frost was not upset to hear that her daughter would be joining the trip because she knew what help Morning Flower had been to the tribe the previous day. She did feel more comforted when she saw that Wandering Bear had packed his things and joined the traveling party as well.

The Chief mounted his horse. The others who were coming along did the same and began to follow him on their way to meet the other tribe. Morning Flower looked behind and waved at her mother. She wanted to assure her everything was going to go well. As she waved she saw Nina walking without a limp or even a bandage on her paw. She looked around and her eyes caught Wandering Bear's as he rode not far behind.

The girl became worried that if Nina would follow the tribe, who was to say that Leaping Ears wouldn't. She searched for a large-eared fox between the horse legs. She hoped not to find her but then saw a black-tipped bushy tail dodge between some horses. Sure enough, the smiling fox had joined them. Morning Flower was unsure how she would be able to protect the fox from the dangers that might lie ahead. Especially since this could be a more dangerous trip than their last one.

As she was thinking of how to shield Leaping Ears her father interrupted her thoughts. "So I notice you have a new friend following you. What is the story behind that?" asked Tall Oak with a hint of a grin.

Morning Flower began to tell of how she met Leaping Ears and how she has followed her ever since but her father stopped her. "I was not only referring to the fox," he said as he nodded his head sideways.

She realized he was talking about Wandering Bear, who was a few feet behind them. She told her father of everything that had happened that past few days and her father was left astonished. Morning Flower received a similar response to the story from her mother.

A few minutes had passed before Tall Oak had his words come back to him. "I understand now why you needed to come. Your mother told me a little last night, but it is so hard to believe that all that happened in such a little time. No wonder Swift Runner looked so tired today," he joked.

He began to ask another question but stopped to listen some more. Time sped as Morning Flower had explained more of her story; they had already arrived at the battle scene quickly. It reminded Morning Flower of the feelings she had when she saw the bison slaughtered just days before. She had been too tired to change into a clean dress the night before and the blood-stained dress she wore now began to irritate her as she looked onward. Not only were there fallen warriors but there were even some horses that were lying lifeless nearby.

Those who came to gather the lost ones began to weep at the sight of them. It was now a fact that they had not survived and the chance of their survival was gone. There was no way now that their loved ones were not just hiding in the field waiting for the tribe to come back and retrieve them. The stench of rotten meat had reached her nostrils as they shooed away the scavengers gnawing on the bodies.

Her stomach began to turn at the scene. *So this is what it looks like after a battle,* Morning Flower thought. She was much younger the last time she had seen such a bloodbath, and yet it looked almost the same. She wasn't sure if she had hoped that the Braves would stand up and walk home or if she had even expected to see them in this motionless state. Now that these images were burned in her mind she was worried about continuing on past the crimson field.

Once the deceased warriors were placed on the travois, the group separated. The women turned and left with the dead being pulled behind their horses on makeshift stretchers. As the others turned to continue towards the neighbor's village, Morning Flower noticed that she was now the only girl in the group. She began to ease Red Storm to slow down. She wanted to be towards the back of the group.

Tall Oak did the same, realizing that it was looking more like a war party now that all the women had left with the exception of his daughter. She tried to reassure him that she wanted to keep going but she began to feel fear creep into her.

Morning Flower was now even more unsure as to why the battle was even caused than before. "Why would they attack our tribe? There was no reason to. We have never fought before and we even joined together at the Powwow a few summers back," Morning Flower whispered.

Her father looked puzzled as well, but then he responded, "Do you remember how the hornet's nests are hidden in the trees and you cannot see them during the summertime? Then when autumn comes, the leaves begin to fall and you see the nests?" Tall Oak asked.

"Yes," she answered.

He began to explain, "It is the same with some people's desires. You may not see them, but that does not mean that their motives are not still there."

Morning Flower pondered her father's words. "I understand, yet I do not," she tried to explain.

Her father replied, "Hopefully we will be able to find out the true meaning behind the attack and not have to wonder much longer."

After they could no longer see the battlegrounds, the Chief pulled his horse to a stop. Everyone dismounted and stretched their legs. Morning Flower tried to hide behind Red Storm and Gliding Feather as Brave Tomahawk began to make his rounds checking on his fellow people. Tall Oak started a conversation with Wandering Bear about random events that were happening within the village to make it appear that he was talking to him the whole time.

But Morning Flowers moccasins and the bright red fox couldn't hide behind the horses' narrow ankles.

Suddenly the Chief recognized the bright roan horse and rushed over to Tall Oak. As his eyes met the startled young girl's, the Chief's voice was filled with anger as he spoke, "Why has she come with us? I thought she was returning with the other group?"

Tall Oak pulled the Chief off to the side and began to whisper to him. Morning Flower's cheeks began to feel warm and it wasn't because of the summer sun. She tried to stand straight but she could suddenly feel everyone's eyes on her. Wandering Bear stood nearby almost as if to shield her from what was to come.

Chapter Eleven

Her father was pointing towards her, the village and even at Eagle Mountain. She knew what he was telling the Chief, but she had never done something this drastic before. If the Chief sent her back she knew that she would have an escort accompany her and she wouldn't be able to sneak away.

She was sure Wandering Bear would volunteer but knew the Chief wouldn't accept this since her father probably just told Brave Tomahawk that he had helped her towards the mountain. She could try to make a break for it but if they caught her she was sure to be punished. Then again, Brave Tomahawk had never said she couldn't come along when they first parted, so it was not as if she had broken a rule directly. On the other hand, his reaction seemed to show differently.

She began to play with Red Storms mane as she waited to hear what was to happen. Both men seemed to have firm faces. Then the Chief walked up to Morning Flower staring her in the eyes. She tried to look away from his piercing face but he demanded her, "Look at me."

She straightened her stance and looked into his dagger eyes. She was sure she felt the same way the children she watched felt when she scolded them for something.

"You will come with us, *but* you will hide once I tell you too. *You will stay* there until I call out to you and for *NO* reason will you leave. Do you understand?" He enunciated his words with care.

She spoke as quiet as she could with him able to hear her, "Yes."

In return he lowered his own voice, bending closer towards her and said, "Your vision has saved many and I am thankful, but do not risk your life any more than needed to today. I will have my eyes on you." With that being said, he stood up and walked to his horse.

Morning Flower refused to look up as her father came towards her. She had never had someone that upset with her, but then again she had never really gotten into trouble.

She tightened her bandage after her father managed to help her jump onto Red Storm. The stallion shook his neck once she was on, trying to get rid of some of the flies that were beginning to pester him. She kept her eyes focused on Red Storm's broad shoulders as he walked behind the group. She said a silent prayer hoping the new dream would mean something, just as the first one did. She had a sliver of doubt try to weasel into her mind as it had done the day before, but she tried to shut it out with the facts she had known. Even though facts couldn't cover up the attention she was getting.

Not everyone in the expedition party knew her story, so some of them began to glare at her. At one point Fire Maker slowed down his own horse to scowl at her, but Wandering Bear maneuvered his horse in between the two and gave a fierce look back at him. Fire Maker nudged his horse and sped up. Morning Flower stopped looking down, lifted her chin up and looked out towards the horizon. She tried to look more confident, her decision to join was already made and she was going to stick with it. She was grateful that she had her father and Wandering Bear to support her right now.

Tall Oak tried to comfort his daughter by telling stories but she didn't focus on them. She was too distracted by her own thoughts. The time seemed to drag on before they reached the border of the neighboring village.

Just then the Chief's horse jogged towards her. As he pointed towards the tree line off to the right as he spoke "You will part with us now. Head towards those trees with your horse and fox and try not to get too close to the village. Once we make our peace, you can follow us back through the trees and meet us back here but no sooner. Do not come out of the trees."

Then Fire Maker spoke up, "What if a battle is to fall? What is the girl to do?" He let out a huff after he spoke.

Brave Tomahawk turned his horse to face the man and reacted, "We are hoping for peace first, remember that." Fire Maker looked sideways to avoid the Chief's eyes. The Chief began to talk to Morning Flower again, but this time in a softer voice, "If the worst does come, you must go through the trees, over the hill and warn our people."

Morning Flower finally looked towards her father; he moved his head towards the direction she should go. Then she nudged the stallion's sides and they disconnected from the group. Leaping Ears followed behind the two but turned her head around to see if they would be followed. When she saw that they weren't trailing them, she pinned her ears back and ran ahead of Red Storm.

Nina began to go with them but once she noticed that Wandering Bear was going with her she sat and gave him a soft whine. He nodded his head towards the three and Nina waited for a moment before the boy waved for her to follow them. She finally trotted as fast as her sore paw would allow letting her catch up with them.

Being in good company, Morning Flower was happy now that the frisky fox and caring wolf had tagged along. As always she was glad that Red Storm was near her also. She leaned forward and patted his shoulder. He replied with a snort and stretched his neck. Morning Flower

212

didn't look back until she reached the edge of the forest.

The group of Braves and horses was still in the same spot

that they were at when she left them. She saw that the Chief

was still watching her as Red Storm weaved between the

first set of trees. Being satisfied that the young girl wouldn't

follow; Chief Brave Tomahawk mounted his horse and led

the way.

Her father seemed to linger longer than the others

until he finally joined the group. Morning Flower tried to

have Red Storm keep up with them but since he had to dart

between trees, bushes and even a few boulders they weren't

alongside the group. Leaping Ears and Nina kept up easily

enough but they all slowed down once the group was

nearing the village.

She urged the stubborn horse to get closer to the

village. Red Storm had felt the tension of the group before

they had left but still could sense Morning Flower's

anxiety. They were still in the trees but would be easily

noticed if someone from the tribe spotted them. The forest grew less dense as they got closer to the other clan's home. The valley would help her hear some of how the talk would go, but she was still unsure whether she would be able to hear everything spoken.

There were things she noticed in the tribe that seemed odd. As Morning Flower looked at the village she saw the remains of a few burnt teepees. Many of the women rushed their children into their teepees as Morning Flower people drew close to the community.

When she saw them doing this, she was drawn to what was laying past the teepees. On the other side, there was a group of… well, she didn't know what they were. They seemed to be made of wood but they appeared to have four circles things holding them up. On top of them, they had some sort of cloth that seemed to be similar to the bison hide that went around a teepee. Looking past these mysterious things, she noticed that two horses had been

214

pulling one of the contraptions. Suddenly a strange looking man came near the two horses and removed them from the object they seemed to be pulling.

She began to worry as she saw the stranger. He looked similar in size of the men in her tribe but his skin was as light as the wheat in the valley. His hair was not black like her own people's but seemed as golden as the sun. Some of the horses from her clan had hair comparable to this man's, but she was unsure of who he was and how he ended up here.

Then she noticed about six more men that had the same colored skin tones as the other mystery man but the hair on their heads varied in color. Some had hair as flaming as foxes, while others had brunette hair like a bison's. She began to worry more and more as she watched them. *What would they do if they saw the men from my tribe coming into the village?*

The men had dismounted their horses before entering the settlement. Brave Tomahawk led his way through the village towards the other clan's Chief. Only the wounded warriors from both bands were visible amongst the teepees. Each side appeared to be clutching their weapons near their sides as they walked closer towards each other.

Morning Flower slid off of Red Storm once she found a well enough hidden area for them all. She lowered herself into the bushes placing her feet carefully not to make a sound. Nina came up from behind, sat near Morning Flower and focused on the scene ahead of her.

Leaping Ears didn't seem to understand that they were trying to keep quiet and let out a playful yelp at Morning Flower. Morning Flower quickly placed her had on the fox's muzzle. Leaping Ears began to understand and crawled on the girl's lap.

One of the men from the Cree tribe had heard the bark though and began to look towards the area the four of them had been hiding. Holding her breath, she dared not move. She clutched the fox closer as the man took a step towards the trees.

Brave Tomahawk had heard the sound from the fox as well and began to speak, the man who was looking for the cause of the noise veered his attention to the confrontation. Breathing began to come back with ease to Morning Flower once he turned. Her Chief sat across from the other Chief and began to speak loud enough that she could hear. "Chief Two Moons, why do you send your warriors to attack us when we were on a bison hunt? We did not cross your area or take from you? What is it we have done to cause such a problem between us?"

The Chief, Two Moons, was a huskier man than her own Chief and had a silver streak in his hair. He straightened his posture and spoke in a deep gravelly and angered voice, "You speak as if you do not know what you did! How dare you come to our village and accuse us of starting the battle, when it was you who did!" Even from where Morning Flower was she could see his nostrils began to flare.

Just then Tall Oak's oldest daughter, Dancing Star, peeked out of the teepee she was in. She whispered as she called to her father.

Tall Oak was relieved to see her, he crept towards her and spoke softly. "Are you alright? Are you hurt? Do you know what's going on?" He asked as quickly and quietly as possible.

She opened the flap a little more and revealed her current state. Her stomach was larger than usual. As her face glowed, her father's heart sank. Not only did he have to protect his two daughters but now another small one was there for him to defend. The little one that grew inside her would be unable to run away from any trouble that might proceed.

Dancing Star was about to speak joyfully about her health but remembered at the sight of the men near her teepee of the circumstances her father was there for. "The tribe thinks that some of your tribe had set our harvest and some of our teepees on fire yesterday morning," she pointed further past the group of men were and where the charred remains had been left as a reminder.

Tall Oak looked with confusion as he saw the scene, "No one from our tribe has left our village besides to go hunting and your sister's trip to Eagle Mountain." He hesitated to continue as he looked off towards the bushes to see any signs of where his youngest child was. "We would have no reason to do this," he stated while shaking his head in dismay.

"That is what I told Fighting Bull but he said the men from our tribe could think of no one else who would do that to us," she replied.

Tall Oak began to look past the group of teepees trying to find any hint of who else could have done such a thing. He noticed, what seemed to be homes, further away on the prairie. Though they didn't look like teepees and the logs seemed sturdy enough for them to shelter someone. There were only a few but he had not seen such strange ways to arrange the poles.

His attention was drawn back to the group of men as they were beginning to get riled up and he began to hurry for any explanations. "What are those logs past the village?" Tall Oak asked.

Dancing Star looked around and tried to clarify, "There have been new people that have come to our tribe. They call it a log cabin. They came about a full moon ago but they look different than you or I. Their skin is bright like the moon with hair that is varied colored like the horse's manes. They have given us many gifts. Our tribe has been helping them set up their own homes, taught them to fish and hunt. But..." she stopped and was drawn to the sound of the conversation that began to rise nearby.

Tall Oak turned his head and heard Fire Maker begin to shout the names of those who had died on the field during the small battle. Brave Tomahawk, who had whipped around to Fire Maker, in a quieter voice said, "You must remain calm as we continue this discussion. We will uncover things soon enough."

She reached for her father's arm, "Some of them are kind while others make me feel uneasy," she finished saying.

Tall Oak patted her hand then left his eldest daughter in her teepee and walked towards Brave Tomahawk. He whispered in the ear of the Chief and pointed towards the other tribe's visitor's living area.

221

Brave Tomahawk, who looked puzzled, asked, "Whatever it is you think we have done, why have you not thought it was those who live over there who might have done the accused crime?"

"Those are our guests! They are the ones who said they saw someone from another tribe set our food supply and homes ablaze!" Two Moons sneered.

"Our tribe would have no reason to do this to a brother tribe. It would be against our way of life to start a war with no motive behind it. You have known us for years. I think you should gather your 'guests' and let us talk to them. Let them see if they noticed any of the men of my tribe. Almost all are here except for those who are seriously wounded or dead," the last of Brave Tomahawks words left a slight sting on them.

"Go and gather them." the Chief Two Moons called to one of his warriors. A younger man turned and raced to the direction where Morning Flower had seen the odd

group of men appear. The rest of the village remained silent

and were glaring down one another until the light colored

skinned men were brought to the gathering by the young

brave.

Two Moons spoke first to one of the men in

particular, "Oliver, this is our neighboring Chippewa tribe."

"How do you do?" the red-headed man, who must

have been the newcomers Chief because he walked with a

sense of pride and importance, smiled as he asked Brave

Tomahawk.

The way he spoke was different than her people as

well. She had heard other tribes speak in different accents

but never one like his. She wondered where these

newcomers had come from. He stepped forward and

extended a hand towards him. Unsure of what to do with

his hand Brave Tomahawk remained silent and stared at the

man named Oliver. Oliver retracted his hand and looked questioningly towards Chief Two Moons.

Two Moons explained, "These are the ones who we fought in battle with yesterday. Which of your men told me that they saw someone from another tribe raid our village?"

Morning Flower noticed that one of the men began to walk backward as if to escape but Oliver called his name. "Abner! You were the one who told the Chief right? You, Hiram, and Lemuel said you saw the event didn't you?"

Morning Flower saw the dark-haired man draw back stammering as he spoke up. "Yes, we did."

"Do you see the man who caused all of this here right now?" Two Moons questioned with confidence that they would find the one who started it all soon enough.

After glancing at the men Morning Flower assumed were Hiram and Lemuel, Abner scratched his facial hair as he looked at each of the men's faces from the opposing tribe with care. He continued looking them over a few times then said, "Mind you it was early morning and dark but I am sure it must have been that one. I wouldn't forget that face." He pointed his fingers and everyone's eyes looked towards the offender.

Everyone turned to see who it was. Wandering Bear looked thinking it would be Fire Maker but everyone was looking at him instead.

"ME?" Wandering Bear asked in shock. He continued but spoke towards his Chief, "You know…" but Brave Tomahawk held up his hand to silence the young boy and everyone from his tribe who had started to grumble. The teenager stood impatiently silent waiting to see how the accusation would unfold.

"Yes that is the one, I am sure of it!" exclaimed Abner, feeding off the other tribe's reaction.

"Yes that is the one we saw as well." replied either Hiram or Lemuel.

Oliver turned towards the three men with confusion on his face, "Is it true that you saw him or was it another?"

The other one who was supposed to have seen the attack said, "No, I am sure of it. It was him."

Abner pushed his cohort aside and spoke with persuasion, "If it was not him it was probably another one who looked similar to him that is not here today. Maybe he died on the battlefield. Who knows but I saw one of them run through the village and torch the tribe's food and teepees. Besides, isn't the fact that your supply is gone fact enough? They came here to fight again. Look at them."

The tribes began to look at each other over with more care. It was hard not to notice the details of those who had worn their war paint and were still stained with the cherry blood from the day before.

"Not when you lie about who it was?" Brave Tomahawk shouted. Faintly calmer he stared Abner directly into the eyes and asked once more, "Are you sure that you saw that young man here yesterday at dawn. If so he will be put to death by my hand for starting this war."

Morning Flower gasped. H*e is a liar! You know he is a liar!* She wanted to shout but her promise to the Chief kept her silent.

The boy was about to speak up again but his Chief hushed him once more. Abner looked over Wandering Bear before he spoke. Wandering Bear sent a warning look back to the man.

"Yes, that is him."

Morning Flower

Chapter Twelve

"YOU SPEAK LIES!" Brave Tomahawk's voice boomed. A loud growl came from her tribe as her Chief spoke. "I know where this Brave was the dawn you speak of and he was not near here. Why would you speak with such dishonesty?!" he was beginning to let his anger unravel.

Fire Maker began to fiddle with the knife that was on his side preparing for a strike. A wave of relief swept over both Wandering Bear and Morning Flower, but the young man knew that it was too soon to be at ease.

Abner was dumbstruck. His face went pale as he fumbled words together, "Wait? If you knew where he was then why ask me? Were you with him yesterday morning?"

"I was not with him but I have others who were and they would not let such lies come out of their mouths especially with someone's life on the line!" roared Brave Tomahawk.

"And you believed these newcomers before trusting us and our people?" shouted Fire Maker towards the other Chief. "Men died because of you!"

Everyone was leaping on their feet and gathering close to one another. Oliver turned towards Abner, Hiram, and Lemuel and began to question them angrily himself.

So much commotion was going on that Morning Flower found it hard to concentrate on one conversation. The clans began to tangle together and the shoving began. When Lemuel tripped one of the tribesmen, he made it seem as if another tribesman was attacking him. This was the snowball that started the avalanche. Everyone was in a yelling match now. Weapons were now being unsheathed, people tried to dodge fists being thrown and blocking knives being slashed.

Morning Flower held her breath, worrying that this war would not end with as few deaths as the battle the day before. Red Storm was beginning to paw the ground with his hooves while Leaping Ears dug her face into Morning Flower's dress. Nina was at full attention as the fight broke out keeping her eyes on only one person.

Morning Flower could hear some of the women and children in the teepees crying as they were blinded by the fight but could still hear the battle developing. The girl tried to cover her eyes, wishing to look away, but the concern for her people won over. The group of quarreling men became hard to recognize. With the shouting echoing down the valley, the group of fair-skinned men that were down by their unknown contraptions stopped whatever they were doing and rushed towards the commotion.

The two Chiefs were arguing with each other, faces full of fury. Oliver was still trying to find out more about the situation from the three men over the turmoil, but they tried to use the chaos to escape the interrogation. At one point a man was thrown into a nearby teepee, the poles that supported the home cracked in half sending the large cloth to fall on whoever was inside. A young woman tried to aid an older woman from the ensnaring fabric and made their way to a safer teepee. The first blood was splattered on the tanned fabric of one of the homes. One man took a broken pole and smashed it across another man's back. Some men had grouped together to beat another man.

Morning Flower frantically searched for any sign of her father and saw that he had found her brother-in-law, Fighting Bull. The two were trying to pull men off of each other but once they released the quarreling men, they were off fighting again. The late afternoon was full of a mixture of war cries and agony being shouted.

Each tribe member was undoubtedly strong so the fight seemed as if it would never end. While one man clung to another's throat as he gasped for air, another would sidestep to avoid the edge of the blade being tossed in his direction. The other tribe tried to be extra careful with the direction they fought. Their loved ones were in their homes near the battle but the closeness of their families also enraged them to fend for them even more.

Morning Flower's eyes caught sight of Abner making his way towards Wandering Bear. Abner ran with his head low and rammed into Wandering Bear knocking the two of them on the ground. The two began to scuffle, gripping each other's fists. Abner snatched a knife trying to stab Wandering Bear as they continued to brawl. Everyone around them was too busy fighting off their own opponent to help.

The knife began to draw closer and closer towards Wandering Bear's heart when he knocked the knife out of Abner's hand. The knife was now too far for either of them to reach. Wandering Bear tried to stretch for the weapon but with the weight of Abner on top of him, he struggled to reach it.

Unable to watch what the outcome would be, Morning Flower stood from where she sat placing Leaping Ears next to her feet. She stood staring at the forest behind her unsure of what to do. Red Storm began to nudge her shoulder with some aggressive force as if trying to get her to leave. Her gut began to ache with endless possibilities. What was she supposed to do?

She remembered Brave Tomahawk's words, "*If the worst does come you must go through the trees and over the hill and warn our people.*" Maybe this was what she was meant to be there for. She stood on a rock to hop onto Red Storm as quickly as she could and began to turn away from the horrific scene until she heard Nina let out a pained bark.

The wolf; who was almost half the size of the horse, ran in front of Red Storm, crouching to stop him from continuing over the hill. She let out a whine and laid her head down.

Morning Flower looked at the wolf with pity. "This is what I am supposed to do. I must warn our people." She lifted her wounded arm and said, "I would only be in the way."

After the wolf sat up, she didn't budge as she stared off into the distance of the furious fight letting out a whimper.

"Stop it, Nina. He can take care of himself. " Morning Flower turned around to take one more glance at her friend in hopes that he was proving that he could fend for himself.

Just then Abner grabbed something from his own side pouch, as he pinned the boy down with his other arm. The metal that was wrapped around the wooden object was shimmering in the light and Abner was aiming it towards Wandering Bear. Nina could wait no longer and suddenly jet off at the sound of her friend groaning as he tried to fight the man off him.

Morning Flower turned Red Storm around and shouted, "NO NINA! COME BACK!" But it was too late; the wolf was out in the clearing racing towards the man who was threatening her companion.

Abner lifted his head as he heard the wolf growling and before she could reach him he raised the pistol that was in his hand. A loud 'BANG!' echoed throughout the valley. Morning Flower clutched her mouth trying to cover her shriek.

"NOOOOO!" cried out Wandering Bear.

Nina lay sprawled out in the field with blood dripping down her fur.

The blast startled everyone, but most still continued their fighting. Wandering Bear became consumed by his anger and fought back even tougher. He was able to get a single blow towards his attacker's jaw. As Abner wiped a trickle of blood from his lip, he hit the boy on the head with the butt of his handgun, leaving Wandering Bear unconscious. Abner began to load something small into the object he had set off on the poor wolf and began to aim it towards the knocked out teen.

Chapter Thirteen

Morning Flower froze in disbelief until she saw a copper object dash across the golden field. Just when Morning Flower couldn't think her heart could feel any heavier, she recognized the snarling fox and her heart nearly stopped. She placed her hands on the stallion's shoulders to brace herself.

Flashes of her grandmother standing up and being shot with an arrow as she fell to the ground and lying lifeless on the snow came before her eyes. Then her dream came back to her with the scenes of the flames gorging themselves on the flowers around her until the single Indian Paintbrush flower glowed radiantly. A desperate tear slid down her cheek as she saw Abner tossed the pistol aside to grab ferrous fox by the scruff of the neck with more ease. Leaping Ears snapped at the man who was clutching her as he still sat on top of the boy. Morning Flower could wait no longer. She gave a firm nudge to Red Storm and he bolted through the trees towards the village without any more hesitation.

"PUT HER DOWN!" yelled Morning Flower.

The raging stallion was at full speed as he galloped and within no time reached the battle scene. Abner seemed slightly shocked but more amused that this girl had come out of nowhere to save a fox in the midst of the battle. Tall Oak and Brave Tomahawk's faces dropped as they saw their no longer hidden clan member was approaching the dangerous scene with such haste. They both pushed their way through the crowd towards her when she shouted, "ALL OF YOU STOP!!!"

The men began to slow down their fists and looked around trying to see who had ordered the command. As the disorder began to simmer down, Abner grabbed raised his pistol with a free hand and aimed it towards the girl when Tall Oak knocked the gun out of his hands just in time.

Morning Flower dismounted her riled stallion and snatched the feisty vixen out of Abner's hand. The small fox gave a gentle lick on her rescuer's face, then turned towards Abner and let out a warning yap. Morning Flower continued to hold the fox as she first went to Nina and saw that the blood was coming out of her front shoulder. The wolf was giving some shallow breaths so she demanded, "Father, come place hold your hand on her wound."

Still clutching the firearm, Tall Oak ran towards the wolf and did as his daughter told him to. The wolf winced with pain but as usual, made no cries.

Abner tried to dodge Morning Flower as she began to walk towards the group of men but Brave Tomahawk stood behind him; with his arms crossed, so the man couldn't escape.

Morning Flower bent down towards Wandering Bear and saw that he was still breathing. Her heart lifted a little as she wiped the small stream of blood from his forehead. She rose to her full height, even though she was the shortest in the crowd she felt like she was towering over him with how much she was raging. Not all the fights had ceased yet, as the group of warriors began pushing their way to get a better view of what was happening.

"You all are fools! You squabble like children and try to kill one another!" she fumed. She glared at the men as they began to halt their fights.

They turned to see who it was that was talking to a group of warriors this way. Some of the men tried to glare back at her but her eyes seemed to burn as fierce as a flaming arrow as she looked directly at each of them.

"Do you think that the cost of this battle is worth the lives you are paying it?" she looked at the fallen warriors that had already lost their lives in the current battle. "You are brothers and yet you turn so easily to fight when someone persuades you too. How? How can you say you bring honor to your tribe when you are willing to fight for a lie and not search for the truth yourselves?"

Looking at her own tribe members, "Do not pride yourselves for coming here to settle this in peace when you know that in your hearts you desired revenge on them. You know you hoped for war. You have no courage! Surely you have no brain either because you did not use it!" The men from her tribe tried to stand straight but were dismayed to be scolded by the young girl.

She caught a glimpse of a sawed-off horn near Abner's side. Brave Tomahawk bumped the man to pay attention and the horn had familiar looking tiny black beads spilling out of a curved bison horn. Realizing what it was she reached into her pouch and pulled out the identical tiny hefty ball she had found just days before. She held it up for him to see as she looked directly at Abner and nearly spat with anger as she spoke. "You started these lies. It was you who slaughtered those bison as well on the prairie wasn't it?"

His eyes showed his guilt even though he was silent and stood his ground.

"Why do you treat our tribe as you treated those animals? Did you not think we would find out how you dishonored them? You slaughtered them and left many wounded without aiding them! Did you thank the Great Spirit for providing you with their lives that brought you supplies? They are not for sport and neither are we! You

243

bring war to our two tribes for what purpose? So we would kill each other? Was it to gain our lands? Our food? To steal what you wanted? Others from your tribe were willing to fight for you but you lied to them as well."

She pointed towards Nina as the wolf continued to lay motionless, "She was protecting him and you wounded her. You might have killed her! You are the one who is causing so much pain and suffering. Do you not stop to see it?" She grabbed Abner's arm and pulled him towards the wolf's face. "Look at her. Look at her eyes! Do you see the pain you caused?"

He tried to break free from her grip and not to look but curiosity won out and he looked into the wolf's eyes as Nina barely glanced up. She let go of his arm and stepped back. "When you look into someone's eyes it reveals a part of them if you look deep enough." She glanced towards Wandering Bear for a brief moment then back towards Abner. "I see it in your eyes now. I see the hatred in them.

244

You must stop spreading the hatred," she said the last sentence with a softer voice.

Looking at Hiram and Lemuel she began to snap again, "Why would you follow someone who is such lies? Who will respect the three of you now that you have done this?" She now looked in the direction of Chief Brave Tomahawk, Chief Two Moons, and Oliver. "Are you not the clan leaders? Should you not have known what to do to protect your people?" The women and children began to peek out of their teepees.

Chief Two Moons was the first to speak back to the teen, "Who are you to think you can talk to us in such a way?"

Brave Tomahawk raised his arm to speak up for her but the girl spoke first, "Who I am is not important, what I am doing is. I am one who thinks for others before she acts."

Brave Tomahawk had a smile of pride begin to spread across his face.

"You allowed war in your camp before you even left the village to battle us," she told Chief Two Moons. Looking at Brave Tomahawk she was saddened to say with as much respect as she could muster, "How would it have been if they started a war in front of your family in our camp? Would you also have gotten protective if he brought Braves painted with war symbols into our home?"

The smile washed off of her Chief's face as he began to ponder over her words.

Not knowing too much about Oliver she glanced at him. "You have traveled far with your men it seems? Do you not know when they lie to you or are willing to bring pain to others? Did you not see any signs?"

Oliver looked towards his men and his mind began to question their motives.

"There will be no more battles between our clans, but you must decide what you will do with those three for causing the deaths of our people and find a way to bring back peace. But remember, they were not the only ones at fault," she noticed that there was a fair-skinned man who had not stirred from the ground. All tribes had lost people that day. She looked towards her father as he continued to aid Nina. She hoped that there wouldn't be another one lost.

"Are you going to listen to this girl?" Abner spoke up. "She is from the fighting tribe. How do we not know-"

Oliver cut him off, "That is enough from you Abner. No more words from you until we sort out what damage has already come out of that mouth of yours."

The men looked around, ashamed of what they saw. Many were covered in blood and others had small wounds. Some fell to their knees realizing that they had killed another man over this meaningless lie. The two Chiefs and

Oliver gathered together. When Abner thought that the attention was off of him, he turned to slip away but Fire Maker stopped him. A few other men including some from the new fair skinned clan gathered around the three troublemakers to make sure they wouldn't leave.

Chapter Fourteen

Numb, Morning Flower stood still trying to figure out if what had happened was real or if it was yet another one of her dreams. She was unable to move as the mass began to bustle around her. Still holding Leaping Ears, the fox nuzzled her neck resting her head on the girl's shoulder and it seemed to finally break the spell that the dazed girl was under. She began to look around spotting any signs of her sister.

She barely recognized her, as Dancing Star came out of the teepee and hobbled as fast as she could towards Fighting Bull. He only had a few minor scrapes as she looked him over. Morning Flower caught the two of them hugging before Dancing Star's eyes caught her sisters.

Dancing Star released her husband and made her way through the crowd towards Morning Flower. Tall Oak stood as his older daughter drew closer, leaving the once again wounded wolf alone for a moment.

"I have never heard you talk so much in my whole life." Dancing Star teased as she squeezed her sister.

The younger sister tried to pay no mind to the joke and saw the new difference to her sister immediately. It was hard for her to believe that she would be an aunt again. Dancing Star grabbed Morning Flower's hand and placed it on her stomach. "The little one was having a powwow earlier."

Tall Oak was glad to see his daughters were alright and hugged the two of them. After releasing his girls and kissing their foreheads he made his way towards Fighting Bull to congratulate him on the addition to the family.

Once her father left, Morning Flower saw Nina still bleeding in the grass and returned her focus towards the injured wolf. As she looked over the wound she noticed in the opening of the wound there was the tiny object in there. "Find me a knife, please." Morning Flower asked her sister.

Dancing Star went towards her husband and grabbed the blade from his side. Before he could reach for it she kissed him once more on the cheek, grinning as she left.

Giving her sister the blade, Dancing Star tried the best she could to sit down next to her. Leaping Ears pushed past Dancing Star, trying to check on her furry friend. She stuck her nose near the wound to smell it but Morning Flower nudged her aside.

Gently, Morning Flower took the tip of the blade and tried to remove the object from the wolf's shoulder. Nina did not make a sound but merely closed her eyes.

Dancing Stars nervously placed her hands on Nina's back to help steady the wolf. After a few slow breaths, Morning Flower had eased the item out and let it sit in her hand. It was a small, now familiar, heavy lead ball that rolled in the warm blood on her palm.

Without a word, Morning Flower rose from Nina's side and went towards the crowd of men that had enclosed Abner, Hiram and Lemuel. With the ball trapped in her hand, the warriors stepped aside as she came near. She grabbed Abner's hand and placed the remnants from Nina's wound in his hand and walked away. She did not wish to look at him anymore or even wait to see his reaction.

Back by Nina, Dancing Star's face was in awe as the unconcerned wolf let herself continue to be petted. Morning Flower was amused to see her sister in this wordless state. Knowing the wolf was in safe care she looked towards where Wandering Bear was. A man was looking over him, she assumed that it must have been one of Wandering Bear's brothers. A few of the men had quickly made some travoises for the wounded or dead warriors. Two men brought one towards Wandering Bear's paint horse and began to saddle it. They then placed Wandering Bear on the travois and came towards Nina.

Morning Flower understood what they planned to do next. She helped them best she could carry the ailing wolf and laid her next to Wandering Bear's side on the logs. Nina nuzzled her head on his arm and gave his torso a tiny lick but Wandering Bear still lay unconscious.

Chief Brave Tomahawk, Chief Two Moons, and Oliver returned to the group after some discussions and spoke of their conclusions to the three tribes' battle. Two Moons spoke first and everyone became silent so that they could hear what the Chiefs' would say. "Our tribe will host our neighbors for the night. We will heal each other's wounds, eat, tell stories, and rest. We will send them on their way back to their homes tomorrow." He bowed his head towards Brave Tomahawk.

"Our tribe will return to Awenasa tomorrow, gathering food supplies and any other provisions we can find and bring them back to our brother tribe. We will help them rebuild what was lost and mend what was broken. We will be stronger now." Chief Brave Tomahawk spoke.

It was Oliver's turn to speak, but when he spoke he looked towards the three who had started it all. "We have also decided that you three will be escorted back East with reports of your actions. Then you will be punished accordingly and it will not be taken lightly. Our group of men will continue further west finding our own valley to call home. Maybe we will visit after our own camp is set up."

Some of the people were not happy with the outcome of the troublemakers' punishment but then again they weren't sure what the outcome would hold for the mischief-makers. At least they would be gone from the tribes. They did know that the three would be heading far east, nowhere near them again.

Wandering Bear's travois was detached from his horse and brought into the village. After some time he woke up startled, thinking he was still in a fight. His brothers told him of what had happened and he noticed Nina cleaned up and bandaged next to him. Morning Flower had finished cleaning Nina while he was still out cold but after he awoke Morning Flower was back near her own family listening to their own tales from the past few days.

That night a few men went and hunted some nearby deer for the dinner. Even with the little food the tribe had left, they were still glad to share it. Some of the women and men from the tribe came towards Morning Flower while she ate and tried to give her small trinkets such as a beautiful bright pink and yellow beaded bracelet but she refused to take anything from them. She felt wrong taking anything after everyone had lost so much.

The tribes gathered any extra bison hides to help Morning Flower's warriors have a peaceful night. Dancing Star arranged her teepee so her father and sister could join them. After a restful night of sleep, she had no memories of any visions and slept until the sun had already peeked over the mountains. Her arm was healing slower than she would have liked. Her body was sore from the previous days of riding but her energy level was back and she felt her mind cleared of worries.

Her tribe packed their few things and said their goodbyes. They would see each other again shortly when they returned with their contributions for peace with the other tribe. A few warriors from the two tribes offered their services to be guides for Oliver and his men as they would go their own way. They would return once they had helped Oliver's group settle.

Morning Flower hugged her sister and brother-in-law goodbye. Tall Oak told Dancing Star that he would try to bring Spring Frost so she could see the good news of their growing family herself. After saying their farewells, the Chippewa Chief led his people on their way home.

Leaping Ears was right on Morning Flower and Red Storm's tail as they made their way back. With Nina not being the lookout, Leaping Ears was more alert than playful on the trip. Morning Flower's father was near her Chief and the two talked, she was unsure whether or not their conversation was about her. So she stayed towards the back of the group once again to avoid overhearing anything.

Still on the travois, Wandering Bear's horse was near Morning Flower as she kept a watchful eye on the injured pair. He was awake now, but stayed on so Nina would be comforted. Leaping Ears jumped on to join them once but without being able to have a clear view she jumped off, unsatisfied with something blocking her watchful vision.

"My brother told me what you did for our tribes. He said you stopped a war by using only your voice. I wish I could have seen the 'Mouse' turn into the 'Grizzly'." Wandering Bear smiled.

"Careful, you said you would not call me that. Plus I will tell Swift Runner you called me 'Mouse' and she might go after you next." Morning Flower joked. "Besides, it was time for me to say something," she said with a more serious side.

"All of your family will be proud," he replied.

The two talked about parts of the story that the other had missed and the trip back home seemed to go quickly.

258

Soon enough they were home and everyone from the tribe knew what Morning Flower had done. Swift Runner nearly tackled Morning Flower when she saw her return. She sat in awe as people talked about what Morning Flower had done. Swift Runner could hardly believe her ears. Before the girls could talk more, Grandfather pulled Morning Flower out of the reuniting crowd and began to walk her towards the hill behind her village.

The defending Leaping Ears and Red Storm refused to leave her side as she walked with Grandfather in silence. She began to recognize where they were heading after they had passed a familiar tree that was bent. It had been some time since she had been there and was unsure why they were going there. Grandfather had brought her to their clan's gravesite. Many small totems were sticking out of the ground marking where each person who had been lost was laid. He led her towards the marker that was her grandmother's.

Though her grandmother died while they traveled and they had to bury her on the trail, once they had settled those who had lost someone made their own graves here. Grandfather stood staring at the totem he had made far too long ago for his beloved wife. Morning Flower did not ask what they were doing but looked silently upon the grave.

Finally, Grandfather moved and reached for something that he had tucked inside his tunic. He pulled out a leather pouch. Curious, Morning Flower tried to guess what was inside but her grandfather spoke.

"When your grandmother showed bravery and stood up for the tribe, they would have honored her with this," he opened the pouch and took an eagle feather from it.

Morning Flower was shocked. An eagle feather was a great honor and rarely given in her tribe.

"Your father told me that the Chief wanted to give you one in front of the tribe tonight, but I told him I would be honored to instead."

Morning Flower was shocked. She couldn't believe that they had even thought about giving this honor to a young girl, especially herself.

Before her mind began to wander too far off, her grandfather spoke again, "I wanted you to remember one place you get your courage from and not have to worry about people. Even though they are all grateful and proud of you." Just then he turned his head and she noticed her tribe standing at the bottom of the hill watching.

She didn't mind that they were watching the ceremony from such a distance. She sat down on her knees and her grandfather held the feather above her head. Then he took a thin strip of leather and tied the feather to a strand of her hair. She stood overlooking her valley and people as

the wind blew her hair and the eagle feather.

How the story began

My parents and I attended a family Thanksgiving in Box Elder, Montana when I was about 10 years old. I remember sitting in the living room with some of the family members sitting around after our delicious dinner. My aunt's family was also there and they have Chippewa Cree heritage. Her father was sitting on the couch near me and he kindly asked me what my name was and I told him my name was Taylor.

He scrunched up his face a little and said, "No. Taylor is a boy's name. You are too pretty to have a boy's name. Can I give you your Indian name?"

Now I love my name because it was at the time, not a common name. I have always been a tomboy so I never minded that it wasn't too "girlie". I looked at my mom to see if she had anything to say and she smiled and nodded her head to reassure me it would be alright.

I told him, "Sure," nervous that I might not like the new name I would be given.

He simply looked me over for a second and said, "Your new name is Morning Flower. A pretty name for a pretty girl."

I instantly loved the new name and ever since then, I have always had the desire to share Morning Flower's story. The tale I felt I might have had if I lived in an earlier time period. I treasure that I have been given such a wonderful name and I am so glad that I am able to share these stories with you.

Characters

Morning Flower- main character.

Swift Runner- Morning Flower's best friend, wishes to become a lookout for the tribe.

Wandering Bear- a boy in the tribe whose best friend is the wolf, Nina

Red Storm- a spirited horse who his loyal to Morning Flower

Leaping Ears- a lively fox who befriends Morning Flower

Nina- the kind but protective wolf of Wandering Bear.

Grandfather- Morning Flower's grandfather also Spring Frost father

Tall Oak- Morning Flower's father

Spring Frost- Morning Flower's mother

Cloud Jumper- Morning Flower's older brother

Wild Dove- Cloud Jumper's wife

Little Duck- child of Cloud Jumper and Wild Dove, Morning Flower's niece

Dancing Star- Morning Flower's older sister

Fighting Bull- Dancing Star's husband

Falling Leaf- Swift Runner's mother

Burning Arrow- Swift Runner's deceased father who was a scout

Crazy Legs- Swift Runner's older brother

Moonbeam- Swift Runner's younger sister

Hunting Moose, Eagle Eye, & Long Knife- Wandering Bear's older brothers

Small Chief- a small boy who is friends with Little Duck, sometimes babysat by Morning Flower

Golden Aspen- Small Chief's mother

Bright Eyes and Mighty Beak- two owls that the teenagers befriend

Gliding Feather- Tall Oak's horse, Red Storm's mother

Sundance- Cloud Jumper's horse

Chief Brave Tomahawk- Chief of the Chippewa tribe

Autumn Sun, Fire Maker- Members of the Chippewa tribe

Kicking Bird- scout for Chippewa tribe

Chief Two Moons- Chief of the Cree tribe

Oliver- the leader of the settlers' expedition

Abner, Hiram, & Lemuel- members of the settlers group

If you'd like more adventures like Morning Flower, Chasing the Prairie Fire please look for the rest of the series soon to be released.

Book 2: Fall in the Valley

Book 3: Roaming during the Bitter Frost

Book 4: Escape through the Mountains

Also more books coming from this author:

Belonging Nowhere

Missing Feathers

Made in the USA
Middletown, DE
22 October 2022

13295031R00163